"I'...

All of her doubts faded away in Macon's arms. Kelly thought she had surely died and gone to heaven, so sweet, so wonderful were his lips on hers. She reveled in the feel of his hard chest, the strong arms that enfolded her. When he broke the kiss, they both gasped for air.

"I want you, Kelly," Macon murmured. With every bit of tenderness he could muster, he kissed her forehead, the tip of her nose, and the tiny cleft in her chin. When he took her mouth again, she was ready for him, and it was a long, hungry kiss that was filled with an urgency that surprised them both.

"I want to make love to you so much it hurts," he said, his warm breath fanning her cheek. "Am I moving too fast for you?"

Kelly thought her heart would detach from her body and fly. Her voice trembled when she spoke. "Maybe just a little," she said finally. She couldn't think of anything she wanted more than to lie in his arms and have him kiss her senseless. But where would they go from there? For she knew that making love with Macon would bind him to her heart forever—and she wasn't certain there was a place in his life for her, and her kids.

"I'd better take you home, pretty lady," Macon said. "Before I show you how fast I can move when I'm sorely tempted. . . ."

WHAT ARE *LOVESWEPT* ROMANCES?

They are stories of true romance and touching emotion. We believe those two very important ingredients are constants in our highly sensual and very believable stories in the *LOVESWEPT* line. Our goal is to give you, the reader, stories of consistently high quality that may sometimes make you laugh, sometimes make you cry, but are always fresh and creative and contain many delightful surprises within their pages.

Most romance fans read an enormous number of books. Those they truly love, they keep. Others may be traded with friends and soon forgotten. We hope that each *LOVESWEPT* romance will be a treasure—a "keeper." We will always try to publish

LOVE STORIES YOU'LL NEVER FORGET
BY AUTHORS YOU'LL ALWAYS REMEMBER

The Editors

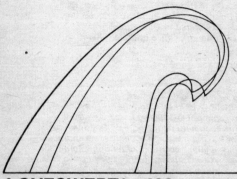

LOVESWEPT® • 433

Charlotte Hughes
Restless Nights

BANTAM BOOKS
NEW YORK • TORONTO • LONDON • SYDNEY • AUCKLAND

RESTLESS NIGHTS
A Bantam Book / November 1990

LOVESWEPT® and the wave device are registered
trademarks of Bantam Books, a division of
Bantam Doubleday Dell Publishing Group, Inc.
Registered in U.S. Patent
and Trademark Office and elsewhere.

If you would be interested in receiving protective vinyl
covers for your Loveswept books, please write to this address
for information:

Loveswept
Bantam Books
P.O. Box 985
Hicksville, NY 11802

ISBN 0-553-44064-0

Published simultaneously in the United States and Canada

Bantam Books are published by Bantam Books, a division
of Bantam Doubleday Dell Publishing Group, Inc. Its trademark, consisting of the words "Bantam Books" and the
portrayal of a rooster, is Registered in U.S. Patent and
Trademark Office and in other countries. Marca Registrada.
Bantam Books, 666 Fifth Avenue, New York, New York 10103.

PRINTED IN THE UNITED STATES OF AMERICA

OPM   0 9 8 7 6 5 4 3 2 1

To Linda—friend, agent, and therapist

One

"Freeze, or I'll blow your head off!"

Macon Bridges halted at the front door, his key dangling from the dead bolt he'd just unlocked. He shot his gaze toward where the throaty female voice had come from, but the room was swathed in murky, abstract shadows.

"Both hands in the air, mister," that same voice ordered. "I've got a gun, and I won't hesitate to use it."

Even as she said it, Kelly Garrett realized it sounded like something from an old late movie. She only hoped she didn't also sound as frightened as she felt. Moonlight wafted through the open door like particles of gold dust, silhouetting the figure of a tall man with sweeping shoulders. Adrenaline gushed through her body; her knees shook and her hands trembled violently. The thought that her sleeping children might be harmed by this intruder was the fuel she needed to confront him in what she hoped was her most menacing voice.

The man raised his hands high over his head. "Look, lady, I can explain—"

"You'll have to explain to the police," she said, even as she wondered how he'd managed to slip past the security gate and gain entrance to the private island in the first place. She groped for the light switch, flipped it on, and they were suffused in light from an overhead chandelier.

This was not your average, run-of-the-mill burglar, Kelly decided upon seeing the man. He looked like he'd just stepped off the cover of *International Male*. Mel Gibson, stand back. His dovegray blazer was unbuttoned, revealing a pale pink and gray oxford shirt. His long legs were encased in a pair of faded denims that hugged his hips and emphasized his trim waist, and had frayed holes in the knees. His beige Reeboks looked as though they belonged in a Salvation Army bin.

"Oh, jeez," she mumbled as her gaze crept up to his face. And what a face! It was the kind of face that made movie stars—lean and weathered from the sun, and framed with thick, dark hair. In contrast, his eyes were stark blue. A slight, almost imperceptible bump along the bridge of his nose, probably from an old break, offered some relief from what would have otherwise been a picture-perfect face. Not that it mattered one way or the other what the man looked like, Kelly reminded herself. He was a lowdown, dirty, rotten criminal. Probably preyed on innocent women and children. That thought frightened her. The last thing she needed to do was let him know she was alone with her three children.

"My husband will be back any moment," she said, leveling her gaze at the man. "He is out walking our two pit bulls, Satan and Killer."

Macon remained perfectly still, but it took every ounce of willpower to keep from laughing out loud. The striking blonde couldn't have been much more than five feet tall. Despite her obvious attempt to appear so, she did not look very formidable. The long T-shirt she wore showed plenty of leg—shapely thighs and calves, gracefully trim ankles, and feet that were as dainty and compact as the rest of her.

"Look, I'm not going to hurt anybody," he said. "I own this place, okay? My name is Macon Bridges."

"Sure it is," she quipped, sounding more brave than she felt. Glancing around, she spotted a long, narrow scarf her oldest daughter had dropped on the floor. She stooped and picked it up. "Turn around and put your hands behind you," she ordered, approaching him cautiously.

Macon sighed heavily but did as he was told. He knew enough about guns to know the one she held was a toy, but he didn't want to frighten her any worse than she already was. "All right, lady, I'll do whatever you want. Is this okay?" He held his hands behind him, crossed at the wrists.

"Eyes straight ahead," she said, slipping behind him. "One false move and you're dead meat."

Kelly stood there for a moment, gun in one hand, the scarf in the other. How was she supposed to do this by herself? she wondered. She rolled her eyes and muttered a four-letter word under her breath. Quickly, she tucked the gun under one arm and began tying his wrists together, glancing at him now and then and praying he wouldn't move. He could have overpowered her easily, but he didn't, and for that she was enormously grateful. She checked the knots and stepped away, holding the gun on him once again.

"Walk toward the kitchen," she said. "To the telephone."

"Now what are you going to do?" He sounded tired and slightly bored.

"I'm going to call the Welcome Wagon and insist they give you a proper reception," she said, sarcasm tinging her voice. "What do you think I'm going to do?"

"Look, before you call the police, would you at least check my identification? My wallet is in my back pocket. There's a driver's license with my name and picture on it."

She heaved a sigh of exasperation. "Persistent to the very end, aren't we? Oh, okay," she said after a moment. "Which pocket?" She stepped behind him once more and reached under his jacket, hands still trembling, feeling for anything that resembled a wallet. Nice firm butt, she thought as her hands skimmed over his hips. Her eyes still trained on him, she reached into the right back pocket of his jeans and pulled out an expensive-looking leather billfold. Probably lifted it from an old lady, she thought, stepping away from him hurriedly.

Kelly flipped open the wallet with her thumb and raised it to her face so she could see the small print on the license. She blinked when she read the name. Macon Bridges. *The* Macon Bridges? she wondered as a sense of dread fell over her. Owner of the mammoth construction company for which she worked? No, it was a trick.

"How do I know this isn't a fake?" she said, looking at him once more. "How do I know you're not an escaped convict? A thief or a serial murderer?" she added, her mind conjuring up an endless list of possibilities. "I think I'd better call the police just the same."

"Check my briefcase," he insisted, nodding toward an expensive-looking attaché case beside the door. "There's a passport inside. And what about the luggage sitting just outside the door? Serial murderers don't cart around luggage."

It all made sense, of course. She edged toward the briefcase and picked it up, but when she tried to open it, she found it locked. "Give me the combination."

He called it out and waited patiently while she opened the briefcase and searched inside. She pulled out the passport and studied the picture, glancing up a few times to look at his face. Her heart sank.

"Oh, Lord, it is you," she finally said. She lowered the gun but couldn't quite meet his eyes. What had she done? Had she really held her boss at gunpoint and tied him up? He would never forgive her for this. He would fire her. She would lose her house. She and her children would be forced to live on the street. She would become one of those bag ladies. Her teeth would fall out.

"If you have any doubts, you can still call the police," he said. "I was just trying to save you some embarrassment."

"Oh, Mr. Bridges, I'm so sorry," she said, shaking her head, "but you are absolutely the last person I ever expected to run into. I thought you were out of the country. Oh, Lord, let me untie you." She hurried over to him and began undoing the scarf. "You must think I'm some sort of kook, but you see, I was all alone with my children and—"

"That's certainly a relief," he said, massaging his wrists once she'd freed him. "I was expecting your husband to come rushing in any moment with those snarling pit bulls at his side."

Kelly blushed. "Well, that's not likely since his new wife keeps him on a pretty tight leash himself." She paused. "I really am sorry, Mr. Bridges." Perhaps if she convinced him how sorry she was, he would at least give her a decent reference when she went looking for another job.

Macon studied the woman before him with unveiled curiosity. She acted as though she knew him, but for the life of him he couldn't place her.

"Have we met?" he finally asked.

"No, we haven't," she said. "I work for you. Or should I say I *used* to work for you," she added nervously. "On the ninth floor in accounting. You were still in Saudi Arabia when they hired me." She held out her hand. "My name is Kelly Garrett."

Macon took the dainty hand she offered and held it for a moment, marveling at the smooth texture of her skin. Her fingers were beautifully tapered, her nails short and painted with a clear varnish. Damn, he had to start going by the office more often. He looked up and found himself gazing into the biggest brown eyes he'd ever seen. He was about to respond when they were interrupted.

"Mommy, I can't sleep," a small voice said from the top of the stairs.

Kelly pulled her hand free and whirled around, at the same time trying to reel in her thoughts. They had scattered in a million different directions as soon as Macon had closed his warm fingers around hers. Nobody had warned her how good-looking or how young he was. She had expected the owner of Bridges Construction to be as old as Colonel Sanders. "Go back to bed, Joey," she told her eight-year-old son. "I'll be up in a minute to check on you."

The boy didn't seem to be listening. His gaze was trained on Macon. "Who is that man, Mommy? And why are you holding my water pistol?"

Kelly noticed the toy gun in her hand and blushed. She had tripped over it coming out of her bedroom and decided to use it. Now she felt ridiculous. "This is Mr. Bridges," she said. "He owns the company where I work." She paused and swung her head back in his direction. "He also owns this house."

"I'm sorry if I frightened you," Macon said. "I just arrived back in the States this afternoon. My secretary said there'd been a cancellation here and that the house was empty this weekend. I should have known better. This place is always full, especially July Fourth weekend."

Kelly knew another moment of dread. She had screwed up royally this time. "My boss, Mr. Hodgins, had originally planned to spend the weekend here, but he had to cancel at the last minute. I was surprised he offered the place to me since I know it's mainly for the . . . uh, executives, and I really haven't been with the company long—"

"Mrs. Garrett?"

"Call me Kelly."

"You don't owe me an explanation. And I'm not going to fire you for protecting your family. That *is* what you were thinking?"

Her cheeks flamed bright fuchsia, but she nodded just the same. She had never blushed so much in her life, and he would undoubtedly think her some kind of bimbo scatterbrain because of it, but at least she still had her job. "It's really nice that you offer this place as a vacation spot for your employees," she murmured, groping for something to say. Then she realized she and her children would probably have to leave now that he'd showed up. "I was so excited when my boss offered it to me that I forgot to clear it with everybody else."

Macon tried not to stare at her expressive eyes or the cloud of blond hair that curled whimsically around her face, or the way her nipples strained against the flimsy fabric of her long T-shirt. "I'm glad you like it," he heard himself say. "Have you been to the beach yet?" He knew he was making superficial conversation while his brain was demanding to know more about her.

"We took a walk on it, but it was too late for swimming." Kelly suddenly remembered she wasn't wearing a robe. Oh, Lord, no wonder the man was staring! She must look tacky as all get-out in her stretched and faded T-shirt. But when she'd heard the noise at the front door, she had bolted out of bed with no thoughts of covering herself. "Would you excuse me for a second?" she said, already backing toward the downstairs bedroom, where she slept. She returned a moment later wrapped in a knee-length bathrobe, just as Macon was setting the last of his luggage inside.

Macon closed the front door, noting the robe with disappointment. The lady had knockout legs. She wasn't any bigger than a mite, but everything was nicely proportioned. Downright sexy, as a matter of fact.

"If you'll just let me use the phone," he said, "I'll call a hotel on the mainland."

"But that's twenty miles away," Kelly said, knowing it would take forever to drive back on the narrow two-lane roads and bridges that linked the islands and connected with the mainland. She shook her head. "No, I insist you stay here tonight," she said, then wondered if *insist* was too strong a word to use with the man who signed her paychecks. "I mean, I would feel a whole lot better if you'd stay," she amended. "You can have my room, and I'll take the spare bed in Joey's room."

Macon wasn't used to taking orders—he normally gave them—but the lady had a point. It was after two in the morning, and the chances of finding a vacancy were slim. Besides, he was fascinated at how the overhead light brought out the gold highlights in her hair.

"I'll agree to spend the night if you'll promise not to move your things from the bedroom," he said. "I can find another place to stay first thing in the morning."

Kelly nodded, too tired to argue. It had been a rough day at work and the four-hour drive along the South Carolina coast had been wearisome with three excited children in the car. She faced her son. "Go back to bed, Joey," she repeated, shooing him up the stairs. "I'll be right up." The boy grumbled to himself but did as he was told.

"I suppose you know where to find everything," she said, returning her attention to Macon.

"I'll manage."

"I'm . . . uh, really sorry about tying you up and all. I was just scared."

He smiled. "I won't hold it against you. Now, go to bed. The sun will be up in a few hours."

She backed away. "Yes, well, good night."

"Good night, Kelly."

She quickly climbed the stairs to her son's bedroom. He had already fallen asleep. She closed the door and tiptoed across the room, pulled down the covers on the spare twin bed and, tossing her robe to the foot, climbed between the crisp sheets. She still couldn't believe all that had happened, but she was asleep almost instantly, exhaustion winning out over her thoughts.

Kelly bolted upright as a shrill, high-pitched scream jolted her wide awake. It sounded again even before she had time to climb out of bed, and she immediately recognized it as belonging to her four-year-old. Fear gripped her as she stumbled from the bedroom in the darkness. She paused long enough to flip on the light at the top of the stairs, then literally raced down them. Behind her she heard her thirteen-year-old daughter call out in alarm.

Kelly had barely reached the ground floor when Katie flew out of the master bedroom, squealing like a baby pig. Macon, wearing navy silk pajama bottoms, was right behind her.

"A man!" Katie screamed, hurling her small body against her mother. "In your bed," she added, among great sobs and gulps. She was obviously hysterical, and couldn't stop jumping around long enough for Kelly to explain.

Macon raked his hands through his hair, feeling confused and disoriented after having been awakened from a sound sleep by the girl's screams. "I don't know what happened," he said. "I was asleep, and all of a sudden I heard all this screaming. I opened my eyes and she was leaning over me, yelling and screaming like a banshee."

"It's okay, Katie," Kelly said loudly, trying to make herself heard over the commotion. She shook the little girl slightly to get her attention, then knelt down so her face was even with her daughter's. "This is Mr. Bridges, honey. He owns this house."

Katie stopped crying long enough to take in the information. She glanced from her mother to Macon and back again. "You know him?"

Kelly noticed Samantha and Joey standing at the foot of the stairs. "Yes, I know him. There was a slight mixup with the house, and he needed a place to stay for the night. It's okay," she repeated.

Katie's small shoulders slumped in relief. "I woke up and it was dark, and I came looking for you," she said. "But when I climbed into your bed I felt all this stuff . . . this fur . . . and I thought it was a bear or something and . . ."

"I'm sorry I scared you," Macon said, coming a bit closer. "I didn't mean to."

Kelly was genuinely touched by the concern in his voice. She glanced up and finally took a good look at his broad chest. It was very furry indeed, she thought, and undoubtedly one of the nicest chests she'd ever seen.

"You're safe, honey," she said to her daughter,

dragging her gaze away from him. "Mr. Bridges won't hurt you." She explained the situation further to Katie, adding that she worked for Macon. Finally, Katie relaxed a bit. She leaned against her mother and yawned. "Feel better?" Kelly asked, and patted her daughter on the head when the girl nodded. Kelly stood, and realized much to her chagrin that she was once again wearing only her T-shirt.

Samantha, who'd been quiet up till now, stepped forward. "I'll take Katie back to bed, Mom,'" she offered. She held her hand out for her younger sister, and after a brief round of good nights, all three children trudged up the stairs together.

"I'm beginning to think we're not going to get much sleep tonight," Macon said, and smiled as though he found the whole thing amusing.

"You and me both," Kelly said, looking down at the floor. It was difficult not to stare at his broad chest and shoulders. "I forgot to mention earlier that my daughter sometimes climbs into bed with me during the night." She paused. "You aren't going to believe this, but usually it's pretty calm around my house at night."

He chuckled. "What d'you say we have a nightcap and try to put it all behind us," he suggested. "I keep a bottle of brandy under the sink. So far, nobody has discovered it."

His smile was infectious, and Kelly couldn't help smiling with him. "I'd like that. Just let me get my robe and make sure Katie is okay."

When she came downstairs a few minutes later,

Kelly found Macon in the living room holding two small glasses of brandy. Thankfully, he was wearing his pajama top.

"Is your daughter all right?" he asked.

"Fine. She's already asleep."

He nodded and handed her one of the glasses. "I don't have any brandy snifters, so we'll have to drink from juice glasses."

"It doesn't matter." Kelly had never drunk brandy in her life. Why should she care what kind of glass it was served in? She raised it to her lips and took a cautious sip. It burned all the way down and spread to her stomach in a welcoming warmth.

"Why don't we have a seat?" Macon said.

She sat down on the bamboo sofa and tucked her feet beneath her as he took the chair nearby. The whole room consisted of bamboo furniture with fat, comfortable cushions, decorated in soothing colors of blue and plum. Watercolors depicting seascapes adorned some of the walls, and one wall had been devoted to an elaborate shell collection placed in small shadow boxes. While the look was both smart and fashionable, it inspired a feeling of relaxation.

So why was she so nervous?

It was him, Kelly decided. True, the last few hours had been unnerving, but Macon Bridges himself was a bit intimidating. Well, more than just a bit. Was this the same man her boss referred to as the "boy wonder"? The man who'd carved an empire from a hole-in-the-wall construction company? Macon's company was one of the most prestigious in Columbia, South Carolina, and employed more than three hundred people. The mere thought made her head spin. Here she was, dressed in her shabby bathrobe, sitting face-to-face with the J. R. Ewing of the construction business.

He cocked his head to one side and smiled at her. "Do all those children really belong to you?"

She nodded; certain the thought would overwhelm him, as it did most men. She probably reminded single men of the Old Woman in the Shoe. "I also have a dog, two cats, and a hamster."

He arched both brows. "I'm surprised you could get away."

"My neighbor is watching them. She's just as crazy about animals as I am. We were both raised with plenty of pets." Even as she said it, Kelly realized she probably sounded dull and uninteresting to a man like Macon Bridges. She wasn't exactly offering conversation he could sink his teeth into. But what could they have in common? They lived in totally different worlds, sort of like Ma Kettle and Donald Trump. He probably discussed things like the stock market and construction business, both of which she knew very little about. Her conversations revolved around subjects like braces, intestinal flu, and cellulite. Exciting stuff to say the least.

Macon found his gaze wandering to her bare feet, which peeked out from beneath the hem of her robe. She had the cutest toes he'd ever seen, the nails painted a soft pink. He was certain each tiny foot would fit in the palm of his hand.

"So you work in accounting," he said, telling himself to stop staring at her toes. "You don't look like an accountant."

And he didn't look like the wizard of the construction industry, Kelly wanted to reply. Macon Bridges didn't build on a small scale, she'd discovered soon after she'd started working for him and saw pictures of his work. He built skyscrapers and five-star hotels in exotic locations, not to mention hospitals and elaborate shopping malls. She had developed a sense of respect for the man before she'd ever laid eyes on him.

How could a man that brilliant look that good? she wondered. And to think, he'd never married. At least that's what she'd heard.

It couldn't be because no woman would have him. She was no expert on men, but Macon Bridges sure seemed like a cut above the herd to her. There was something about him, an underlying sense of strength and self-confidence and, yes, masculinity, that made her very much aware of herself as a woman. And the effect he was having on her was almost scary. She had to get out more, she told herself. All those Saturday nights she'd sat home with her kids was obviously taking its toll. She'd forgotten how to act in front of a man.

"So how was your trip?" she asked, thinking it best to try to appear intelligent to the man who held her career in his hands. He wasn't going to have a whole lot of confidence in her as an employee if she sat there making goo-goo eyes at him all night.

He shrugged. "Tiresome. I don't like to travel. I always get behind at the office when I go away. And now I'm being forced to take a couple of days off. I could get a helluva lot done this weekend at work with people gone."

"Forced?" she repeated, surprised. "Somebody actually had to force you to come to this magnificent house on the ocean?"

He nodded. "Doctor's orders. I'm supposed to relax and bring my blood pressure down. It's not really that high, but my doctor says it could get high if I don't take it easy." Macon frowned. "He worries too much. I've always been in perfect health. But last year he made me stop smoking and told me to get more exercise."

"And did you?"

"I stopped smoking, but I don't really have time for a regular exercise program. I don't have time to do the things I like to do, much less those I don't like."

"What do you like to do? In your spare time, I mean?" Though Kelly was not a particularly shy woman, she was not particularly nosy, either. Yet for some reason, she was compelled to learn as much as she could about this man.

"I enjoy photography," he said. "I used to be good at it, won a few awards, as a matter of fact. I still carry my camera around with me—I brought it here this weekend—but I seldom find time to use it."

"You have to make time," she said. "Believe me, I've learned from experience."

Although unasked-for advice usually irritated Macon, he found himself leaning forward in his chair toward Kelly, eager to continue the conversation. He even acknowledged that what she said was quite sensible. "I feel guilty when I'm doing things strictly for pleasure, though," he confessed. "I feel like I'm wasting time, goofing off."

She nodded. "I know what you mean. With three children, it's almost impossible for me to find time for myself. I make myself take it. Even if it's fifteen minutes in the bathtub with my favorite magazine. But don't worry. Once you dive into that ocean tomorrow, you'll forget all about work."

Macon chuckled as he sat back. It wasn't likely. His schedule the past few weeks had been grueling, and he'd found himself gulping down two or three glasses of brandy at night to relax. But now, thanks to the pretty lady, he was beginning to unwind. She was easy to talk to. "So you're divorced?"

She nodded. "My husband married a woman he felt could enhance his career. Guess that says a lot about me, huh?" She grinned and took a sip of her drink.

"And did she?"

"She must have. They bought a house last year in one of those hifalutin subdivisions where you have to pass through a security gate to get in. I think it's mandatory to drive a BMW. You can imagine how embarrassed they are when I pull up in my old Buick with three kids in the backseat."

Kelly stared down at her glass, amazed at the things she was telling the man. Maybe it was nerves. She talked incessantly whenever she was anxious. She was also having trouble making eye contact with him, and not just staring. He was probably used to women gawking at him, she consoled herself. Even more distracting than his good looks, she was awed by the fact that he owned the company where she worked and was rolling in money. He'd probably never shopped a clearance rack in his life, she thought dismally.

Deciding to quit while she was ahead, before she did something really foolish and really lost her job, Kelly stood and carried her unfinished drink into the kitchen. She could feel Macon's gaze on her as she poured the brandy down the sink. When she turned to leave, his large frame loomed in the doorway. The kitchen suddenly shrank in size.

"That wasn't very frugal of you," he said, motioning to her empty glass sitting on the counter. "That brandy costs twenty-five bucks a shot."

Kelly stared at her glass. Lord, that would have filled the gas tank in her car. Then she tilted her head back and met his blue-eyed gaze. His easy smile softened his features, giving him an unexpected boyish appearance. But this was no boy. The silk pajama top strained against his powerful chest. Coarse black hair peeked out over the buttons he'd undone. She caught the faint scent of sandalwood and spice.

"Anybody who can afford to pay twenty-five dollars for one drink, " she said, "can certainly afford to waste it." Where had that glib reply come from? she wondered. Her insides were churning and vibrating as badly as her old washing machine on spin cycle.

He folded his arms over his chest and leaned against the door frame. "I like you, Kelly Garrett."

She liked him, too, heaven help her. She liked those jewellike eyes and that handsome face. She liked the low, husky pitch of his voice and the way he listened to her as though he was really interested in what she had to say. And she liked the firm lines of his body. In fact, there wasn't much about the man she didn't like.

"I'd better get to bed," she said, reminding herself once again who she was gawking at. "My youngest has a tendency to rise with the chickens."

Macon knew a moment of disappointment. He would have enjoyed talking with her some more. But she did look tired. "Thanks for sitting up with me."

Sleep did not come right away for Kelly. Every time she closed her eyes, she saw Macon's face. She found herself wondering what he would look like in a shower with water sluicing down that gorgeous body, and she buried her head beneath her pillow in an attempt to block the image. She was obviously turning into some kind of sex maniac. But she really liked the man, darn it, and he'd said he liked her.

Don't kid yourself, she chided herself silently. The man is way out of your league.

Macon was too wound up to go back to sleep. He hung his clothes neatly in the enormous walk-in closet and stacked his sneakers on the overhead shelf. He was meticulous with his clothes, a habit he'd picked up in the old days, when he'd only had one outfit to his name. Nowadays, he spent more on a suit than most people spent on a used car. It was part of the image he'd developed long ago—one had to look successful in order to be successful. Of course, he'd always tried to look his best despite having no money. Even in high school, when it had been fashionable to wear worn and tattered jeans, he'd opted for neat slacks and a crisp shirt. He'd gotten his first job at age twelve, and every spare dime went for clothes.

Only now, now that he could afford the best, did he feel comfortable in his old jeans. In fact, he preferred them.

He was about to close the door when he spied Kelly's clothes hanging on the opposite side of the closet. He retrieved a delicate-looking sandal from the floor and marveled at its smallness. She couldn't weigh more than one hundred pounds soaking wet, he thought, smiling, but the lady was a powerhouse of energy and presence. Warmth and a sense of caring radiated from her, a tangible thing. He'd felt it pass between her and her children as they'd stood there in their pajamas. It evoked tender images in his mind, a slender white hand touching a feverish cheek, draping an old-fashioned quilt across a child on a blustery night. Those same hands stroking a lover . . . his gut tightened at the sudden turn his thoughts had taken. The mere idea of those hands on a man's body, *his* body, stoked a fire low in his belly.

The images were confusing and almost frightening in their intensity. She was part Madonna but still very much a woman. And yet, she possessed girlish qualities that he found endearing. She was open and honest, and he liked that. And while she appeared independent, he was certain she would never make a man feel as if he weren't needed. She was the kind of woman who inspired men to pick wild flowers and give up their jackets on a cool night; yet he knew she could be strong enough for both of them if she had to. Macon wondered how he could possibly know these things after having only just met her. It was odd, this feeling of kindredness.

He grabbed his briefcase and slipped between the cool sheets that still carried Kelly's sweet scent. It had become a habit of his to fall asleep over a mountain of paperwork, although earlier he'd dropped off surprisingly quickly. He stared at the contracts before him, but couldn't concentrate on them. All he could think of was her. He decided then and there he would have to get to know her better.

Two

When Kelly opened her eyes the following morning, she knew she'd overslept. She blinked several times, trying to clear her groggy brain and reacquaint herself with her surroundings. A shaft of sunlight peeked through heavy draperies, patterning a gold design on plush carpeting. She could hear waves crashing on the beach outside.

She glanced at her son's empty bed and bolted upright, suddenly remembering how close the ocean was to the house. Snatching up her robe, she stuffed her arms into the sleeves, then ran from the room and stumbled down the stairs.

She heard her children talking in the kitchen and sighed with relief. When she entered the room, she found them sitting at the table with Macon.

"Good morning," she said breathlessly, combing her hair from her face and pulling her robe closed. "I'm sorry I overslept. Did my children wake you?"

Macon smiled at Kelly, adorably disheveled and making every effort to pull herself together. He was certain she had no idea how lovely she looked, or how utterly desirable. "No," he answered. "The telephone started ringing before seven o'clock."

"What on earth for?"

"Business." He stood and crossed the room to the automatic coffeemaker. He'd sat up most of the night reading. In fact, he hadn't fallen back asleep until almost dawn, and had been wakened shortly after by the telephone. Oddly enough, he felt rested. He'd learned a long time ago that he didn't need eight hours sleep like most people. He got by on a lot less. "How do you like your coffee?" he asked as he filled a mug for her.

"Huh?" Kelly hadn't heard a word he'd said. Her gaze was fastened on his trim behind, which she thought looked absolutely heavenly in a pair of khaki shorts. His legs were long and finely muscled and feathered in black hair. Covered enticingly by a knit shirt the color of his eyes, his shoulders and chest were just as wide as she remembered. Reminding herself not to gawk, she forced herself to look at his face. He was watching her, staring actually, his gaze fixed on her lips. She licked them nervously.

"My coffee?" she said dumbly. "Oh. Just black." She accepted the mug from him. "Thanks."

"I hear you're quite a bear until you've had your coffee," he said, leveling his gaze on her once again. He felt uneasy with her, and the feeling was a new one. His self-confidence had always been a driving force in him. But this lady was different from anyone he'd ever met, and he couldn't seem to keep his eyes off her.

Kelly cautiously sipped her coffee. "I see my children have been gossiping about me." She glanced at the group around the table, who were munching on toaster pastries she'd brought from home. "Don't believe anything they tell you. Now, what's this business with the telephone? I thought you were supposed to be on vacation." It wasn't until then that she noticed his briefcase opened at the kitchen table, papers scattered all around it. She pursed her lips and shook her head.

Macon shrugged as he refilled his own cup. "I'm used to it." He turned to gaze thoughtfully at her. She was still flushed from sleep, and her shoulder-length hair tumbled about her face in a flattering way. He was suddenly reminded of a young girl on the verge of womanhood who was still a bit unsure of herself and had absolutely no idea what she did to men. Desire stirred in his body, surprising him. Kelly Garrett really wasn't his type.

"I called a realtor this morning," he said after a moment, "who handles island rentals. This place is packed for the weekend."

"Then you'll just have to put up with us," Kelly said, and she tried to appear calm about the whole thing. But the idea of Macon Bridges sleeping under the same roof with them and sharing their simple fare was enough to make her break out in hives. "Surely you can stand us for two days," she added, forcing a brightness to her voice she didn't feel.

"If you're sure you don't mind."

"Then it's settled."

Macon was relieved to have that over with. He had hoped she would invite him to stay, but he hadn't wanted to intrude on her time with her family. Thankfully, she didn't seem to mind.

"Can we go to the beach now?" Katie asked.

"You didn't finish your Pop-tart," Kelly said.

"I'm not hungry." The girl scooted from her chair and headed for the trash can to dump her plate.

Macon stopped her. "Here, let me wrap that up for later," he offered. "No reason to waste it. You might want a snack when you get in from the beach."

Kelly watched in bemused silence as he wrapped the partially eaten Pop-tart in aluminum foil, then checked Samantha's and Joey's plates, as well, for leftovers.

Kelly studied her reflection in the mirror. Although her one-piece suit was modest by most standards, it still showed plenty of skin. The top was strapless and fit snugly against her breasts, while the legs were cut high on her thighs. She wasn't model material, she decided after a minute, but she would do. She was thankful she'd gotten into the habit of riding her bicycle with the kids on weekends in an attempt to firm up before summer. After slipping into her terry-cloth jacket, she joined her children, who waited in the living room.

"All ready!" she announced. The kids whooped and raced for the sliding glass door that faced the ocean. As she followed, Kelly noticed Macon at the dining room table with his briefcase before him. "Have you got that thing handcuffed to your wrist, or what?" she asked.

He looked up, his expression blank. "Did you say something?"

She shook her head. "I was just wondering if you wanted to join us on the beach."

"Oh, well, I thought I'd catch up on some of this paperwork."

She planted her hands on her hips and shot him a look of pure exasperation. "You're on vacation. How many times do I have to remind you?"

He smiled sheepishly. "I'm afraid I don't know much about vacations. Maybe I'll join you in a little while."

She doubted it. "Then would you mind carrying out this ice chest of drinks when you come?" she asked, motioning to a small Styrofoam chest.

He leaned back in his chair, gazing at her with amusement. "Is this your way of making sure I show up?"

"You catch on fast, boss man." She smiled and let herself out the sliding glass door.

An hour later Macon strode across the hot sand wearing a pair of faded cutoffs. He stopped suddenly when he spotted Kelly in her bathing suit, feeling as though his head would blow off. She might be small, but the good Lord had not omitted one single curve in designing her.

"I *like* that suit," he said as he joined her.

Kelly blushed to the roots of her hair. Her fingers automatically sought the bodice of her suit and pulled it higher on her breasts. "Uh, thanks," she mumbled, refusing to look at him. Her gaze stayed fixed on her children in the surf. "I see you decided to join us after all."

He grinned. "Did I have a choice?"

She returned the smile, trying to keep watching her kids when what she really wanted to do was stare adoringly at that chest her daughter had described as "furry." "I was going to get you out here one way or the other," she confessed. "I feel I owe it to the company."

He set his lounge chair beside hers and sat down, still taken aback by the sight of her—as well as his body's potent reaction to her. "Your ex-husband is an idiot," he said, then realized he'd been thinking out loud.

Kelly whipped her head around in surprise. His gaze was hot and intent. Another furious blush scalded her cheeks. Suddenly, she wished she were a snail and could crawl inside her shell and hide.

Macon didn't miss the rosy blush. "I didn't mean to stare. Am I embarrassing you?"

"Yes. Very much."

"I'm sorry. I just never expected a mother of three to look like you do. You're full of surprises,

Kelly Garrett. But you're probably accustomed to men staring."

She managed to meet his gaze. "Not really. Between my job and my children, I don't get out as much as I should. So if I don't seem as witty and . . . sophisticated as most women you know, you'll have to forgive me." She blanched as the last words tumbled out of her mouth. Now, what had made her go and say something like that, for heaven's sake? And to her boss of all people! But every time she compared herself to the type of women she was sure he was used to being around, she came off feeling boring and matronly. Instead of looking offended by her remark, though, Macon looked amused.

"You underestimate yourself, lady." After a moment he went on. "I've said it once and I'll say it again. I like you, Kelly Garrett. You're easy to be around. Comfortable. I can relax."

She pondered his words. He could have been describing a good recliner, she thought with disappointment. She didn't want Macon to feel "comfortable" with her. She wanted to excite him, shake him up a little, just as he was doing to her. That wasn't likely, though. She had no illusions about herself. She looked every bit of her thirty-three years, and had a thirteen-year-old daughter to attest to her approaching middle age. Tiny stretch marks from her pregnancies marked her stomach, and she had developed laugh lines and crow's feet in the past couple of years.

What could a man like Macon Bridges possibly see in her?

"Have dinner with me tonight?" he said softly.

She couldn't have been more shocked by the request, and actually gaped at him. "Are you inviting me and my children or just me?" she asked.

"Just you. You said you don't get out much. It'll do you good."

"I don't have a baby-sitter."

"I'm sure Samantha won't mind sitting for a couple of hours if we ask her."

"I don't know, Macon." What on earth would they talk about? She would bore him to death with mundane conversation. They didn't have the first thing in common. "Why me?" she finally asked.

"Why not?"

"Because you're my boss, that's why. And because we're so . . . different." She didn't feel she had to list the differences. They were glaringly apparent to her.

"Our professional life has nothing to do with this," he said matter-of-factly. "Besides, I enjoy being with you."

That was the clincher. She enjoyed being with him too. And she was darn flattered that he'd asked her. She would just have to try to forget who and what he was, at least for one evening. "Of course I'll go," she said. "Thanks for asking me." She would make witty dinner conversation if it killed her, she told herself, even if it meant having cue cards printed up in advance.

He smiled, obviously pleased. "Tell you what," he said, checking his wristwatch. "I've got to make a couple of phone calls—"

"But you just got out here," she objected. "How are you ever going to enjoy your vacation if you spend your time running back and forth to the telephone?" She didn't wait for him to answer. Instead, she held out her hand. "Give me your watch."

"I beg your pardon?"

"The wristwatch. Give it to me."

"I've grown quite fond of it, if you don't mind."

"You can have it back when we leave. But as long as you're here, I refuse to have you checking the time every five minutes." Was refuse too strong a word? she wondered. "I just wish you'd try to forget about business for a little while."

"You're serious, aren't you?"

"Darn right I am. Besides, it makes me nervous every time you check your watch. I keep thinking I'm supposed to be somewhere . . . at my gynecologist's office or something."

He chuckled, but handed over the wristwatch nevertheless. "Masterful, aren't we?"

"I'm going to see that you follow your doctor's orders to the letter," she said firmly. "Even if I have to toss this watch into the ocean and unplug the telephones."

He was still smiling. "Why do I get the impression I've lost control of my life?"

"I'm doing this for your own good. You're going to thank me one day."

•   •   •

Once again, Kelly studied her reflection in the full-length mirror. She had changed clothes three times. The white slacks and navy and white striped blouse was one of her nicest outfits, but she was still unsure. She glanced at her daughter. "What do you think?"

"Mom, stop worrying," Samantha said, eyeing her mother's reflection. "You look fine. Besides, it's not like you're going on a real date. Macon is probably just trying to show his appreciation because you let him stay."

Kelly's shoulders slumped. "Thanks, Samantha, I needed that," she said dryly.

"I didn't mean it like that. I just meant—"

"Never mind." Kelly held up both hands. "If you say anything else, I might not have the nerve to leave this room."

"Want some woman-to-woman advice?" Samantha asked, giving her mother a conspiratorial look. "Go without a bra."

Kelly's mouth dropped open. "Samantha Garrett, I'm going to pretend I didn't hear that."

The girl giggled. "Aw, c'mon, Mom, get with it. You want to get his attention, don't you?"

"Not if I have to strip down and do a bump and grind routine. Besides, I work for the man. I certainly don't want to make a bad impression." She reached for her purse and drew out her lipstick. "Now, promise not to leave the house while I'm gone," she said once she'd applied the coral shade to her lips. "I don't want your brother and sister near the water."

"I promise. Just go and have a good time."

Kelly shot her daughter a suspicious look. "Why are you being so agreeable to baby-sitting? You've never been this eager before."

"That's because you never pay me, Mother. Macon is giving me five dollars an hour. And believe me, I need the money. You should try living on my allowance." She opened the bedroom door and motioned for her mother to pass through first. "Don't want to keep Macon waiting."

Kelly found him sitting on the sofa, dressed in a pair of dark slacks and a white pullover that emphasized his tan and made him look downright sexy. She had fed her children earlier and promised to take them for a walk on the beach when she returned, so they could watch the fireworks display.

"All ready," she said, and was pleased with the appreciative glance he shot her. She kissed Joey and Katie good-bye and gave Samantha one of her I'm-counting-on-you looks before going out the door. Macon ushered her to his Mercedes.

"You look great," he said once he'd joined her in the front seat, "and you smell better than apple pie."

He didn't look and smell so bad himself, she thought. "Keep talking like that and you won't have to buy dinner."

They conversed easily as Macon made the short drive to the next island. A few minutes later he pulled into the parking lot of a weathered screened-in building called the Seafood Shanty. "It doesn't look like much, but the food is great," he said.

The restaurant's screen door squeaked loudly as he pulled it open. Kelly stepped inside and looked around. Tables for anywhere from two to eight people were set in rows across the plank floor. About half were occupied—mostly by families —and the air was heavy with the enticing aroma of cooking seafood.

"It smells wonderful," she said as Macon led her to the window used for ordering. She glanced up at the blackboard menu. "What do you recommend?"

"Everything is good. I usually get the fried stuffed shrimp."

She nodded. "That sounds good to me."

"Okay, why don't you get us a table, and I'll order. This place fills up fast."

On the other side of the restaurant she found a table for two that looked out over the marsh. It seemed to spread out for miles. On the opposite side of the highway, several shrimp boats chugged slowly into the inlet, returning with their day's haul. Sea gulls circled the boats, several perched on the riggings, no doubt hoping for some supper.

Macon carried a tray overflowing with food to the table and set it down. He handed Kelly a glass of iced tea and took another for himself. Once he'd unloaded the rest of the tray, he put it aside and sat down.

"It looks fabulous," she said as he set her plate

in front of her. Realizing how hungry she was after a day on the beach, she bit into a piping-hot hush puppy. She'd never tasted anything so good.

Although Macon enjoyed his dinner too, his gaze was constantly drawn to Kelly. Her face and shoulders were pink from the sun, giving her a lovely, healthful glow. Her blond hair looked squeaky-clean, pulled back from her face with combs that resembled seashells. Every so often he caught the scent of her perfume. It didn't overwhelm like some. Instead, it teased him and made him want to bury his face against her breasts and inhale her fragrance.

"You're staring at me," she said. "Do I have ketchup on my face?" She reached for her napkin.

He chuckled and shook his head. "No, I was just admiring your new tan."

"Is my nose peeling? It always peels, and then I get a million freckles."

"I like freckles."

"Then you came to the right place. Now, stop staring at me or I'll crawl under the table and never come out."

"You need to get used to men staring at you, Kelly," he said, his voice taking on a serious tone. "You're a beautiful woman."

"And you're a sweet-talker, Macon Bridges."

He arched one dark brow. "I never say anything unless I mean it."

She didn't know how to answer, and was thankful when he turned his attention to his dinner. It was impossible to chew with him staring at her like that. She'd already bitten her tongue twice because of it.

After dinner Macon grabbed a to-go bag for Kelly's leftovers and drove to a nearby fishing pier. Holding hands, they walked the length of it, conversing with people along the way. Kelly watched the salty wind whip through Macon's dark hair as he chatted with a man about the kind of bait he was using. She couldn't say she'd been making the wittiest conversation all evening, but at least she'd avoided talking about intestinal flu. And Macon seemed to be enjoying himself. She certainly was. And that worried her.

"Let's make a date for tomorrow morning," Macon said as they arrived back at the house. "I want you to watch the sun come up with me."

She stared at him. She'd spent the entire drive wondering if he'd kiss her good night—and how it would feel if he did—and instead he asked her to get up to watch the sunrise?

"What time are we talking about?" she asked suspiciously.

He grinned. "Very early."

"You want *me* to get up at some ungodly hour to watch the sun come up? Can't you just snap a picture of it and let me see it at ten?"

He reached for her hands. "No, you have to be there to appreciate it. The sun looks like a big orange ball. It's the most beautiful thing in the world." He paused as he studied her face. "Well, almost. What d'you say? I'll knock on your bed-

room door when it's time. I'll even make coffee.
And you can go back to bed afterward if you
like."

As they walked to the house, Kelly pretended to
give him a hard time about rising so early on her
day off, but she knew she would climb out of bed
at any hour just to spend time with the man.
"Okay," she finally said. "Don't forget, I take my
coffee black."

At the front door he paused. "Thanks for dinner, Kelly. I had a great time."

"Me too," she said, and meant it. For a little
while she had forgotten he was the top dog where
she worked, and she had been able to enjoy herself. Except for the times she'd caught him looking at her, *really* looking at her. Her insides had
turned as soft as spun taffy.

Even though she'd wondered about it, she was
not prepared when his lips brushed hers lightly,
like an ocean breeze caressing her skin. He tasted
wonderful, but the kiss was over before she knew
it, leaving behind the scent of his aftershave. When
he opened the door, Samantha was waiting for
him with a list of telephone calls, all of which he
said looked important. Kelly didn't bother to invite him to join her for a walk on the beach with
her children. He was still on the phone when they
returned, poring over papers in his briefcase, and
he hadn't gotten off when she climbed into bed
sometime later.

• • •

The next morning Kelly tried to ignore the steady pounding on her bedroom door as she slipped farther beneath the covers. Macon had insisted she take the master suite, and he had moved to the spare bed in Joey's room.

"C'mon princess," he called out from the other side of the door. "It's showtime."

She peered out from her covers and saw that it was still dark. "Go away," she mumbled. "I've changed my mind."

Macon chuckled. "Make yourself decent," he said. "I'm coming in."

She bolted upright in the bed, dragging the sheet to her breasts as the door swung open. "But I'm not wearing makeup!" she exclaimed.

"Oh, for heaven's sake," he muttered, picking his way across the dark room. "Here's your coffee. Now, hurry. Sunrise is in eleven minutes."

She yawned wide and accepted the coffee cup. "How can you possibly know that? I took your wristwatch, remember?"

"Don't try to wheedle out of this, young lady. We made a deal. Where's your bathrobe?"

"Foot of the bed."

He fumbled near the end of the bed and felt a tiny foot. "What's this?"

"Katie climbed into bed with me during the night," Kelly said, trying to talk around another yawn. "But then, you already know about her tendency to do so."

"It should make for an exciting sex life." He found the robe and handed it to her.

"What sex life?" she grumbled.

"Exactly."

With only a little fumbling, Kelly managed to get the robe on. "Okay, lead me to this sunrise," she said. "And I'm warning you, it had better be good."

The sky was a mixture of grays and mauves as Macon led her out to the picnic table in the back-yard that faced the ocean. Waves slapped against the sand, and the salty breeze whispered through the grasses and fluttered the sea oats that grew sparsely along the sandy ridge. Overhead, orange fingers reached from behind the clouds, announcing the first rays of sunrise.

Kelly's gaze was fixed on the sky where the sun appeared, first as a blinding sliver of light. A kaleidoscope of color surrounded the sliver as it grew to a great fiery ball, illuminating the sky for as far as she could see. Before long, the sun hung low over the water like an enormous orange Christmas ornament. "It's really beautiful," she whispered. In fact, it was breathtaking.

"I almost fell over the first time I saw it," Macon said, gazing across the ocean too. "This is a far cry from the neighborhood I was raised in."

She was surprised at the confession and told him as much. "I sort of got the impression you came from a wealthy family," she said.

"Not at all." He smiled ruefully but didn't elaborate, and she didn't press him. She was certain Macon Bridges would divulge only what information he wished, especially where his personal life was concerned. But knowing that he'd worked to get where he was made her see him in a whole new light. She returned his smile, thinking he must have trusted her in order to tell her what little he had.

For a moment they stared at each other. When his lips captured hers, Kelly was more than willing to go to him. She snaked her arms around his neck and pulled him closer, and for a moment she forgot everything else. He was no longer her boss, a man of power and wealth. He was simply a man, sexy and virile and wonderful to be near. The feel and smell of him was unlike anything she'd ever experienced. It left her slightly intoxicated. His tongue slipped between her lips and gingerly explored her mouth, stealing her breath. When he broke the kiss, she could only gaze at him in wonder.

"I'd like to see you after we get back," he said, and smiled at the look of surprise on her face.

"I'm not sure that's such a good idea," she said. "Our lives are too different. And you don't really know me."

"I know enough."

"Did you know that I'm always juggling five things at once and that I can be moody and bitchy sometimes because of it?"

"Yes, your kids told me."

"My lifestyle would drive you crazy," she went on, talking more to herself than to him. "Everywhere you look there are kids . . . my kids, the neighbors' kids. And animals. Not only my own, but every stray within a ten-mile radius. I spend most of my time trying to find homes for them. My house is always cluttered, and I can't keep up with my chores. You'd go stark raving mad."

"That sounds wonderful to a man who has always felt shut off from the rest of the world."

"Macon . . ." She paused, trying to gather her thoughts and think of a nice way to say what was really bothering her. "I need my job. The salary is good, and I have great benefits."

"Thank you," he said, taking her comments as a compliment. "We try to be competitive. But what does that have to do with what we're talking about?"

"I just don't want to foul up things at work, that's all. If you and I were to start seeing each other, I'm sure there would be talk. And if things went wrong between us, I'd be very uncomfortable working for you." When he didn't say anything, she continued. "I felt pretty crummy about myself after my divorce, Macon. It's been three years now, but I still have bad days. This job makes me feel good about who I am, and I need that in my life right now. I just can't risk messing it up."

He gazed at her with surprise and disbelief. "Why, Kelly, I would never interfere with your job. What makes you even think it?"

She glanced away, realizing how ridiculous she must sound to a man like Macon Bridges. "Some men would," she said softly.

"Why, for heaven's sake?"

She shrugged, wishing she had never brought it up, wishing she could take it all back. "I think some men feel threatened. Not you, perhaps, but some. If a woman develops too many outside interests or becomes successful, some men try to sabotage those efforts."

"I can't imagine why. Unless the guy is a jerk, and he's afraid the woman will discover it if she gets out in the world and meets decent people." He looked at her for a moment, a half smile playing on his lips. "You don't think I'm a jerk, do you?"

She laughed. "Of course not. But what about my coworkers? How do you think they're going to react when they find out we're seeing each other?"

He sighed heavily, but amusement glinted in his eyes. "You know, it doesn't have to be this difficult. We're friends, so what? What can they say? And why should we care one way or the other what they say? We can't spend our lives trying to please everybody we meet, you know. Besides, most people don't care anyway."

It made sense, of course. And Macon made everything sound so easy. "I'd like to think about it," she finally said.

He seemed to accept her answer, and Kelly *did* think about it much of the day as they lazed on the beach. Afterward, the entire group chipped in and cleaned the house for the next family who would be arriving that evening. Kelly tackled the refrigerator, and found herself tossing out bits and pieces of food that Macon had saved and wrapped in aluminum foil. She unwrapped a half-eaten pickle and gazed at it thoughtfully. Why would a man like Macon Bridges hoard food? she wondered. The same man who paid twenty-five dollars an ounce for brandy. She shook her head and tossed the pickle into the trash.

Kelly's mood was glum, and the children bickered constantly on the drive back to Columbia despite Macon's promise to stop with them at their favorite restaurant for dinner before going home. The last fifty miles seemed to drag for Kelly, and all she could think about was getting her brood to bed.

They arrived at the house late, and she had a million things to do to get ready for work the next day. Macon stayed only long enough to drink a glass of iced tea, and Kelly was certain he couldn't wait to get back to those papers in his briefcase. On the way out he bumped into her best friend and neighbor, Margie, in the process of returning Kelly's pets. The woman patted her short red hair self-consciously as Kelly made introductions. Then Macon was gone, climbing into his Mercedes and driving away.

Margie's mouth was still hanging open as she followed Kelly into the house. The children were in the next room hugging their animals.

"I want to hear all about it," Margie said. "Don't leave a thing out." Kelly obligingly filled her in on the events of the weekend as she unpacked.

"Are you going to see him again?" Margie asked. It was obvious she was excited. Margie had been divorced almost twice as long as Kelly and was always full of advice. She couldn't understand why Kelly didn't date more.

"He says he wants to see me," Kelly began, "but I don't know if it's wise since I work for him. You know how sticky those situations can get. Besides, if you saw how addicted he is to his work, you'd understand why I'm not getting my hopes up."

Kelly had barely gotten the words out of her mouth before Joey yelled for her at the top of his lungs. They almost collided in the hall.

"My hamster got out of the cage!" he cried.

Kelly went into action. "Quick, find the cats and get them out of the house!" She ran full speed down the hall to her son's room, then dropped on her hands and knees beside the bed to search for the animal. Life as she knew it had returned to normal.

Three

Three days had passed since Kelly had last seen Macon, and her mood had steadily worsened. Served her right, she told herself time and again. He'd said he wanted to see her, and she hadn't gotten very excited over it. At the time it had made perfect sense not to get involved with him, but she hadn't counted on missing him so much.

It was after eleven o'clock on the third night when, having decided she would never fall asleep, Kelly left her bed and took everything out of her kitchen cabinets. She was in the process of wiping them with a damp cloth when her doorbell rang, waking her miniature dachshund and sending him into a fit of barking. Kelly almost fell on the floor when she saw Macon's face on the other side of the peephole.

"Hi," he said as she opened the door.

She blinked at him. "Long time no see," she said blandly, but her stomach was pitching wildly. Finally she realized her dog was climbing up Macon's legs and pulled him away.

Macon didn't seem to notice the animal. "I tried to call several times," he said, stepping through the door, "but the line was busy. I figured it was Samantha on the line with a boyfriend." When Kelly didn't say anything, he went on. "I got called out of town the night we got back. There was an accident at the Galveston site, nothing serious, thank God, but I had OSHA people crawling all over me for a couple of days. Luckily it wasn't our fault, but it got our attention." He paused and shrugged as though he couldn't figure out why she wasn't saying anything. "I even tried to call you at the office, but you were out to lunch."

"Nobody told me."

"I didn't leave a message. I figured you'd prefer it that way. I drove over here as soon as my plane got in. Hope you don't mind."

"Of course not." She tried to smile, but her bottom lip trembled at the effort. The fact of the matter was, she had thought she'd seen the last of Macon Bridges. She had wrestled with indecision for three days about whether to see him again, and had come to the conclusion that it was a moot point since he obviously had no intention of calling her. She had felt betrayed, as though he'd snatched the decision right out of her hands by not contacting her. Now she felt ridiculous. He'd simply been called out of town for an emergency, something beyond his control. But she had conditioned herself to think the worst for so many years that it was hard to break the habit.

"Is something wrong?" he asked when she said nothing more.

"No. Everything is fine." Actually, she was thrilled to see him. All her doubts faded as she led him into the kitchen. He looked exhausted, she noticed. Deep lines bracketed his mouth.

Macon glanced around the room and saw the empty cabinets standing open. Dishes and pots and pans filled the counters and kitchen table. "What's all this?"

"Huh?" She followed his gaze. "Oh, I was just cleaning out my cabinets. I couldn't sleep. Would you care to join me for milk and cookies?"

"If you don't mind. I know tomorrow's a workday for you."

She shrugged. "It doesn't matter." She didn't bother to tell him about the bouts of insomnia she'd suffered since coming back, a direct result of meeting him. It didn't matter if she was in bed or not, her eyes refused to close. She took several crunchy peanut butter cookies from a tin and put them on a plate, then poured two glasses of milk.

"Why don't we sit in the den?" she suggested, handing him his glass. "That way we can catch the end of the news."

He followed her into the next room and joined her on the sofa. When she offered him a cookie, he took one.

"They're good," he said after his first bite. "Did

I tell you the other day I liked your house? It looks like it belongs on a Christmas card, all cozy and lived-in." He studied the room as he talked. One wall had been devoted to pictures of her family, another held framed artwork that her children had done. The coffee table was stacked high with books and mail. A coloring book lay open, the page only half finished.

"I warned you my house was cluttered," she said. "You should see my laundry room."

"It's a nice clutter. Are the kids in bed?"

She nodded and offered him another cookie. He took the plate from her and set it aside, then pulled her against him. "All I want to do is hold you for a minute," he said. "I missed you, Kelly Garrett. I missed having coffee with you in the morning and watching the sun come up. I even missed hearing the kids argue. Does that surprise you?"

"A little."

He chuckled. "It surprised me too." He gazed at her thoughtfully for a moment, wondering if he should kiss her. But he had absolutely no idea where their relationship was going or if she would even welcome his kiss. "So this is your dog?" he said, trying to change the direction of his thoughts. He glanced down at the animal, who seemed to be waiting for somebody to pay him a little attention.

"He'd better be," Kelly said, "because I've been feeding him for years. This is Runt, and he's spoiled rotten." She had no sooner gotten the words out of her mouth than the black and tan dachshund sat up on his hind legs. Macon laughed and rubbed the dog's head.

"The cats sleep in the garage," she added. "I got tired of them sharpening their claws on my draperies, so I kicked them out."

Macon tried to act interested, but it was impossible not to stare at her delicate face and the cloud of blond hair that looked as soft as goose feathers. "What have you been doing while I've been out of town?" he finally asked.

"Working mostly. I have a girl who comes in to stay with the kids while I'm gone, but I always come home for lunch to check on them. Katie's back in dance, and I just signed Joey up for Little League. Samantha is spending a productive summer on the telephone."

Macon toyed with a fat blond curl as she spoke, wrapping it around a finger. It shone under the lamplight like spun gold. Unable to resist, he nestled her closer and tucked her head beneath his chin, catching the scent of her shampoo. It smelled like wild honeysuckle. Damn, it felt good to be with her, to feel her softness. She was nice and curvy, a pleasant change from some of the women he'd dated who were so fashionably thin, they at times appeared anorexic.

Kelly glanced up at him. She'd never admit it, but being held like this by him was one of the most pleasant sensations she'd ever felt. With some effort she forced herself to continue the conversation. "And what has been going on in your busy life?" she asked.

"Well, we're bidding on a convention center near Houston. I flew over there once I got things squared away in Galveston. Actually, it's like a country retreat, designed with a Victorian flair, with hundreds of acres of land for golf and horseback riding and tennis courts. The main buildings will have huge wraparound porches and beveled windows and fifteen-foot ceilings."

"It sounds beautiful."

"You want to see the blueprints?" he asked, looking almost boyish in his excitement. He even appeared less tired. "I have them in my car."

She nodded enthusiastically. "I'll pour you another glass of milk while you get them. Or perhaps you'd like a drink. I think I have a little wine in the fridge."

"Milk's fine," he said, already heading for the door. He returned a few minutes later with a stack of blueprints, made room on the kitchen table, and dropped them there. "This is the main hall," he said, unrolling one. "Get a load of that staircase. They want it built of solid mahogany. No expense is to be spared."

Thirty minutes later they were still poring over the blueprints, Macon pointing out details that would have otherwise escaped Kelly's attention. She could not help but notice the energy and passion that flowed through him as he spoke of his work. It was obvious the man loved what he did. No wonder the doctors couldn't get him to take a break.

"Lord, look at the time," he said at last, glancing at his wristwatch. He yawned, then began rolling up the blueprints. "My lawyer and a bunch of stodgy old bankers are coming to my house first thing in the morning, and you have to get up early for work." He looked apologetically at her. "I shouldn't have kept you so late. If you're as tired as I am . . ."

"I'm glad you did," she said.

He slipped his arms around her waist and pulled her close. "I wish I didn't have to leave," he murmured, his voice low. "But I'm going to be at the office tomorrow, so maybe I'll see you."

Kelly almost laughed out loud at the thought. The building where they worked consisted of fifteen floors, half of which were used by his construction company, and the rest leased to other firms. It was not likely they would run into each other at the copying machine or the coffeepot. But she didn't bring that to his attention.

"Oh, by the way," he said. "A friend of mine is having a dinner party at his house Friday night. Would you like to go?"

She didn't have to think twice. "Sure. What should I wear?"

He shrugged. "You look good in everything. I'll pick you up around seven, how's that?" She nodded, and he checked his watch again. "I have to go."

He gazed at her a moment, then without warning tilted his head down and kissed her. Kelly stood perfectly still as he enfolded her in his arms, drawing her close against his wide chest. His mouth was warm and gentle, yet firm. He coaxed her lips apart and explored her mouth with a thoroughness that left her trembling. Nothing in all her thirty-three years had prepared her for such a kiss. It was mind-boggling, consuming. All she could do was hang on for dear life.

When Macon released her he was smiling. "The whole time I was gone I thought about kissing you."

So had she. "It was kind of nice, wasn't it?"

"Yes, it was." He suddenly threw his head back and heaved an enormous sigh. "Damn, I hate to leave," he muttered. His expression of frustration and desire confirmed his words. Nevertheless, he released her and gathered up his blueprints. She followed him to the front door. "Don't forget to lock up," he said, pausing to drop a brief kiss on her mouth.

"Good night," she murmured, and closed the front door. She locked it, then returned to the kitchen to turn off the lights, feeling as if she were on a cloud. She spotted the dishes on her cabinet and frowned, then decided she would put them away in the morning. She just wanted to think about Macon for a while. The doubts that had plagued her for three days now seemed meaningless.

Kelly drummed her fingers on her desk, eyeing the telephone and willing it to ring. She had placed a call to Macon's office an hour before, giving his secretary the impression it was company busi-

ness, and although the woman had said she expected him back any moment, Kelly had not heard
from him. Now she was beginning to wonder if
Macon's secretary had forgotten to give him the
message, or if it was lost in a mountain of paperwork
on his desk.

Another thought struck her. What if Macon's
secretary had figured out the truth, that Kelly was
simply using business as an excuse to get through
to him. She blanched at the thought. Everybody
on the executive floor could be having a big laugh
over it right now.

"Get a hold of yourself," she muttered under
her breath. She was growing paranoid. The people on the executive floor didn't even know she
existed.

The executive floor. Macon's world. Kelly couldn't
help but wonder what it was like. Her boss had
promised to take her on a tour when he'd hired
her, but they'd never found time. Of course, her
boss went up there all the time for meetings. He
was up there right now, as a matter of fact.

Suddenly, it was irresistibly important that she
see this part of Macon's life. She had called to tell
him she wanted to see him again, but how could
she make such a decision without knowing all the
facts about him? Since she was opening herself
up for a possible relationship with the man, didn't
she have a right to know how he lived and worked?

She glanced at the stack of telephone messages
that were awaiting her boss's return. Shuffling
through them quickly, she saw nothing earth-

shattering. But wait. How about this call from his mechanic who said his tires needed to be rotated? That looked important. Her boss would surely want to act on it right away. And frankly, she didn't want to be held responsible for any catastrophe that might occur as a result of his not following his mechanic's expert advice.

With her decision made, Kelly grabbed her pocketbook and slung the strap over her shoulder. She only hoped she wasn't making a mistake.

At the elevators she punched the up button. A minute later the doors on one slid open soundlessly, and she stepped inside, edging her way between several important-looking men carrying briefcases. She pressed the button for the twelfth floor and realized her hands were trembling. She took a deep breath to calm her nerves. If she suddenly chickened out, she could pretend she'd punched the wrong button.

A tiny bell sounded as the doors swished open, revealing the twelfth floor. Kelly stared at the sight before her. It was nothing like she'd expected. It didn't resemble an office at all. It looked more like the lobby at the Hilton. A man behind her cleared his throat discreetly, and she realized she was holding up the elevator. She tossed him a confident smile and got off just as the doors started to close. She had reached the point of no return.

She stood motionless for a moment, feeling as though she'd just landed in Oz. The furnishings were unlike anything she'd ever seen, highly polished mahogany and brass and comfortable-looking

couches and chairs covered in obviously expensive fabric. She felt tacky and very much out of
place in her simple maroon skirt and white cotton
blouse. She should have worn her navy suit.

"May I help you?"

If Kelly had felt ill at ease before, it was nothing
compared to the feeling that hit her when she
found herself looking into the unsmiling face of a
security guard.

"I'm . . . uh, looking for someone," she said,
faltering for a reply. "But I don't see him, so I
think I'll just . . . uh, leave." She turned for the
elevator.

"Perhaps I can find him for you," the guard
replied. "What's his name?"

She blinked. "His name?"

The guard frowned as though he were growing
impatient with her. "Yes, his name."

"Frederick, is something wrong?"

Kelly turned around at the sound of the female
voice. Standing behind her was a smartly dressed
woman with perfectly coiffed hair, looking as
though she'd just stepped off the pages of *Vogue*.
Yes, Kelly told herself, she definitely should have
worn the navy suit.

"This lady says she's looking for someone," the
guard said. "I asked her his name, but she refused to tell me. Lady, perhaps you should give
me *your* name," he added to Kelly, "and tell me
what you're doing up here."

"Kelly, is that you? What are you doing here?"

Kelly paled at the sight of her boss hurrying

toward her with a stack of loose papers in his arms. She suddenly wished the floor would open up and swallow her as she realized how utterly dumb her excuse for being there was going to sound.

"Oh, Mr. Hodgins," she said, her face heating as she groped for an explanation. It had all sounded so convincing when she'd practiced it in her mind at her desk. She would just waltz up to the executive floor, hand over the messages, and get an eyeful of the world in which Macon wheeled and dealed. She hadn't counted on her boss looking so busy or these other people acting so suspicious and impatient. But wasn't that the way things always turned out when a person plotted and connived and told untruths to get what she wanted? Her involvement with Macon was already leading to a life of subterfuge.

"I have your telephone messages, Mr. Hodgins," she said at last.

He looked slightly alarmed. "Is there an emergency?"

"Uh, not exactly. But your mechanic called and said your tires needed to be rotated and, well, I thought you should know." She felt faint as the three merely stared at her, apparently expecting something more. She would undoubtedly go down in history as the yardstick by which all fools were measured. "I was on my way to lunch and thought I'd just drop these off," she added.

"So you know this young lady?" the guard asked her boss, who nodded in return.

Kelly didn't hear the elevator doors open or see the men in dark suits file off. But she did sense Macon's presence, and when she saw him surrounded by all those important-looking men, she wanted to crawl into a crack and hide the instant those blue eyes collided with hers.

"Kelly honey!" he exclaimed when he spotted her. He strode over, a bright smile on his face. "What are you doing here?"

Her mouth went bone-dry as Mr. Hodgins and the security guard gaped at her. "I . . . uh—" She paused, feeling as though the whole world had suddenly stopped turning. It reminded her of the E. F. Hutton commercial where everybody in the room stops what they're doing and stares at one person. She wanted to die. "I was on my way to lunch and—" She paused again. Did she really want to go through the whole spiel about her boss's tires and have Macon and his colleagues give her the same funny look she'd just received from the others?

"That's right," Macon said loud enough for the whole group to hear. "We *were* supposed to have lunch today, weren't we? It completely slipped my mind." He slapped an open palm against his forehead as though he couldn't believe he'd forgotten. Kelly wanted to throw herself at his feet and thank him for preserving what dignity she had left. "I don't know why you put up with me," he added, shaking his head. The men with him nodded sympathetically, as though to say they'd done the same thing a dozen times before.

Macon took her hand and squeezed it, then handed her over to his secretary, the *Vogue* model lookalike. "Hannah, would you please show Miss Garrett to my office . . . and give her a cup of coffee while I finish some last-minute business. Oh, and call the Steak and Chop House and make reservations for two." He turned back to Kelly. "Just make yourself comfortable, honey, and I won't be long."

With that he was gone. Flanked by the men in dark suits, he disappeared through a massive door which Kelly suspected led to a conference room. She did not miss the look of absolute surprise on her boss's face as he stepped inside the elevator. He was still staring when the doors slid closed.

"Miss Garrett, would you come this way, please?" Hannah said, smiling warmly at Kelly and acting as though the last five minutes had never taken place. "And thank you, Frederick," she said to the guard curtly, dismissing him. He muttered something under his breath and took his place near the elevators.

"Please forgive us for being so rude," Hannah went on as she led Kelly across the expansive reception area. "Frederick is retiring at the end of the year, thank heavens, but in the meantime we have to tolerate his disagreeable ways. Ah, here we are. This is Mr. Bridges's office. Just make yourself at home. What do you take in your coffee?"

"Just black, please," Kelly said weakly. Hannah nodded and left, closing the door quietly behind her.

For a moment all Kelly could do was stare at the sheer opulence of Macon's office. She was certain the room would fit right in at the White House. "Oh, what have you done, Kelly?" she mumbled. "You don't belong here. This man is way out of your league." How many times had she told herself that? she wondered. But being there confirmed it. Macon's world was utterly foreign to her. She had no business in his life.

The door opened a few minutes later. "Here we are," Hannah said, carrying a teacup filled with aromatic coffee. Kelly accepted the cup, noting that it was fine china, a far cry from the tacky souvenir mugs they used in accounting.

"Is there anything else I can get you while you wait?" the woman asked. When Kelly shook her head, she disappeared again.

Kelly sat on the leather sofa, overly careful not to spill her coffee on the carpet, an off-white knotty-textured blend that must have cost more per yard than her monthly mortgage payment. She continued her perusal of Macon's office, noting the wet bar that covered half of one wall, and another wall devoted entirely to books. Several framed pictures decorated the remaining wall space, most of them completed projects, she noted when she got up to study them more closely. Some of the pictures showed Macon in the foreground, surrounded by handsomely dressed men and women.

"What do you think?"

She hadn't heard him come in, and whirled around at the sound of his voice. Coffee sloshed over the side of her cup. Thankfully, it landed on her skirt and not the carpet.

"Macon, I'm so sorry," she said breathlessly.

He quickly took the cup from her and set it on his desk, then grabbed a tissue and began mopping the front of her skirt. "What on earth for?" He glanced up at her, obviously confused by her distress.

"For coming up here like this. I should have known better. I just—"

He tossed the tissue away and slipped his arms around her waist. "You just what?"

He smelled wonderful. Woodsy. "I just wanted to see you."

His lips grazed hers. "I'm glad you came. I'm glad you wanted to see me bad enough to brave the likes of Frederick the Troll. I never meant to put a guard up here, but some of my executives are puffed up with importance and have grown paranoid as a result." He smiled intimately. "I wanted to call you this morning, but I ran out of time. Now, how about lunch?"

She checked her watch. "Macon, my lunch hour is almost over. I'm afraid I don't have time. My boss will be expecting me back at one o'clock."

He turned to his desk. "I'll ring him up and explain the situation."

"Please don't," she said as he picked up the telephone. At his look of surprise she went on hurriedly. "I'm a bit behind. I'd better just get back." It wasn't altogether true, but the last thing she wanted was Macon using his position to win favors from her boss.

He seemed to sense that, and hung up the telephone. "But you have to eat."

"I'll grab a hot dog from the vending machine."

"Then I'm going with you." He cupped her elbow in his palm and ushered her toward the door despite her protests. "I promised you lunch, and I'm going to see that you eat. Now, stop arguing."

They bumped into Hannah as they were leaving the office. "Your reservations are in fifteen minutes, Mr. Bridges," she said.

"Cancel them, please, Hannah. We're going to grab a hot dog from the vending machine." He smiled broadly, as if the thought delighted him, and Kelly guessed he hadn't eaten many meals like that.

Hannah merely smiled and nodded as though it made complete sense. "Certainly, sir. Enjoy your lunch."

When they reached the first floor vending area, Macon reached for his wallet. "Is there a change machine down here?" he asked, thumbing through several crisp bills.

"Just for one-dollar bills," she said.

"Damn, all I have is a couple of twenties."

"And a Gold Card," Kelly said woodenly, noting the various credit cards in his wallet.

"I'll get change from the cafeteria."

"No, you'll have to wait in line forever." She opened her purse. "I'm sure I have some singles. It's the story of my life." She fumbled through her wallet and pulled out several crumpled bills. "Here, allow me to buy lunch today," she said, attempting to smooth them out so they would go into the change slot.

"I don't want you to have to do that, Kelly."

"Don't be silly. This whole harebrained idea was mine in the first place."

He stuffed his wallet back into his hip pocket as he watched her make change. "It wasn't harebrained. In fact, you just turned a very dull afternoon into a helluva good time."

That pleased her immensely, and she smiled as she dropped a handful of change into one of the vending machines. "Okay, what do you want? Ham and cheese, tuna fish—" She frowned. "Looks like they're all out of hot dogs."

"Do they have peanut butter and jelly?"

She laughed. "No, I don't think so."

"Darn, I really had my heart set on it."

"How about roast beef? I can make you a peanut butter and jelly sandwich later."

"When?"

She glanced up. "When do you want it?"

He planted one hand on the vending machine and leaned close. "I want it now," he said, a wicked gleam in his eyes.

Kelly blushed a bright red. She wasn't sure they were talking about the same thing. Every nerve in her body snapped to attention. Energy seemed to flow between them like an electric current, making her arms and legs tingle.

"Macon, I have only a few minutes left on my lunch hour," she finally managed to say, her voice trembling. "Now, be a good boy and tell me what kind of sandwich you want." She should have gone home for lunch as she always did, she thought. She would have saved herself a lot of embarrassment.

"Would you bring it tomorrow?" he asked, his mind still fixed on the peanut butter sandwich. "We could walk to the park and eat it there."

"If I promise to bring you one, will you choose something out of this machine?"

"And we'll need potato chips. I like sour cream and onion. I'll furnish the drinks."

"Yes, Macon," she said between gritted teeth as she noticed a group of women she worked with walk by, looking at her as though she'd just sprouted horns. She sighed. Well, her fears had come true. All her chickens had come home to roost. She had made her bed, and she was going to have to lie in it.

"Then I'll take the roast beef," he said.

She pressed the necessary button; the sandwich slipped from its slot and fell with a dull thud to the bottom of the machine. She chose the same for herself. "We'll have to share a soft drink," she said, counting the rest of her change.

"Is this table to your liking, madam?" he asked, ushering her to a round, waist-high table. There were only three in the room.

"Fine." She no longer cared where or what they ate. She just wanted to get it over with.

"What are you doing after work today?" he asked before biting into his sandwich.

"I've got to drop Katie off at dance and take Joey to ball practice. How 'bout you?"

He grimaced. "I have a dinner meeting with some OSHA people. I should be finished by ten. Mind if I drop by for milk and cookies?"

She met his hopeful gaze. "I suppose it's okay," she said after a moment. That meant she would have to hurry home and load all the dishes back into her cabinets. She had missed her chance that morning when she'd overslept. That reminded her, she *had* to stop by the store and buy a new alarm clock. She couldn't count on her old one anymore, which explained why she'd overslept and had almost been late for work.

Speaking of late. She checked her watch. "Oops, I've got to go," she said, reaching for her napkin and dabbing the corners of her mouth.

"But you didn't finish your lunch," he protested, pointing to her half-eaten sandwich. "Aren't you going to wrap it up for later?"

"You eat it."

"Don't I get a kiss?"

She gave him a look that told him she seriously questioned his grasp of reality. He shrugged and asked, "What time should I meet you tomorrow?"

"Twelve o'clock. Why don't we meet here?" she suggested. "I don't think I'm up to another confrontation with Frederick. If it's all the same to you, I'd prefer staying away from the executive offices."

"Most women like it."

"I'm not most women."

"I know. That's what I like about you."

She hurried to the elevators and managed to squeeze herself in among the crowd before the doors closed. Back on the ninth floor, she would have been blind not to notice the stares from some of her coworkers as she walked down the hall to her desk. She bent over to cram her purse into a bottom drawer, and when she straightened, her boss was behind her.

He was smiling. Actually, he looked very amused. "Did you have a nice lunch, Kelly?" He didn't give her time to answer. "You know, I had planned to give you a tour of the executive offices myself, but it's probably old hat to you by now."

"I can explain—"

He chuckled. "No explanation necessary," he said, giving her a fatherly pat on the shoulder. "Just take care of yourself around those bigshots. They eat people like us for breakfast. I hope Macon Bridges knows what a lucky man he is. Also . . ." He leaned closer. "You'll be relieved to know that my tires are being rotated as we speak." He winked. "I certainly didn't want you to lose any sleep over it."

Kelly managed to smile. "Yes, well, we should all rest better knowing that."

Four

"Okay, Margie, how does this dress look? But before you answer, I'd better tell you this is the only thing I have to wear that's really nice."

"I like it."

"You're just saying that. I shouldn't have told you it was all I had." Kelly turned to the full-length mirror and studied her reflection. The dress was a simple pale pink shift with padded shoulders and white bib collar. "Does it look home-made?" she asked.

"It looks like you bought it right off the rack, Kel. Nobody will ever know you made it on that antique sewing machine of yours. What are you so worried about? It's only dinner."

"Yes, but I have no way of knowing what the others will be wearing, and after what I went through yesterday . . ." Kelly let the sentence drop.

She had told Margie about her visit to the executive floor, and Margie had gotten a huge kick out of it. As for herself, Kelly failed to see the humor in it and had considered not going to the dinner party with Macon. But they'd had such a wonderful time eating peanut butter and jelly sandwiches that afternoon in the park, she'd decided to go after all. In her heart she knew there wasn't much she wouldn't do to be with him.

"Will you help me with my makeup?" she asked. "You always do such a good job."

Margie rolled her eyes but went into the bathroom, where Kelly kept her makeup. Instantly, she poked her head around the door. "When did you decide to wallpaper the bathroom?"

"Sometime after midnight last night," Kelly said as she stepped out of the dress and pulled on her bathrobe. "I couldn't sleep. I bought the paper a long time ago but never found time. You'd be surprised how much I'm getting done these days because of my insomnia."

"Does this problem with sleep have anything to do with the new man in your life?" Margie asked, searching through Kelly's makeup drawer.

"It has everything to do with him." Kelly sank onto the bed and shook her head. "I don't know what he sees in me."

"Oh, brother," Margie muttered.

"It's true. He could have anybody."

"That's right, but he obviously wants you. You should feel on top of the world, girl."

"I feel so inadequate. If you had seen his office

yesterday . . . And I can only imagine what his house looks like." She glanced around her bedroom. "This place looks like a nightmare compared to what I saw yesterday."

. Margie sat next to her on the bed. "That's not really important, Kel, and you know it."

"What if I embarrass him in front of his friends tonight? What if I'm not as . . . sophisticated?"

"Maybe he likes you that way. Have you ever considered that possibility? Now, do you want me to do your face or not?"

The telephone rang, but Kelly didn't move to answer it, knowing Samantha would snatch it up instantly. A moment later the girl appeared in the door way.

"Mom, that was Macon on the telephone."

"Good, he's canceling. I don't have to put myself through this."

"No, he said to tell you he's been held up at a meeting, and he's sending a car for you in an hour. He'll meet you at the dinner party."

"You only have an hour!" Margie exclaimed, scrambling to her feet. "We'd better get started. We still have to do your hair. Let's go into the kitchen, where the light is better."

Kelly sat at the kitchen table as Margie instructed, but it was all she could do to keep her disappointment from showing. She was getting dressed up for her first real date with Macon, and he couldn't take the time to pick her up. It was silly, she supposed, but she'd fantasized over it all day, what he'd say, how he'd look at her when she opened the front door and he saw her for the first time. She'd cleaned her house in record time, putting out fresh apple spice potpourri so it would smell nice. And now he couldn't be bothered with leaving his precious meeting early and driving across town to get her.

An hour later Kelly studied herself in the bathroom mirror, flanked by Margie and Samantha. She was determined to make the best of the evening. "Don't you think I have on too much blush?"

"No," Margie said. "I've told you three times you look great."

"You do look fantastic, Mom," Samantha said, "and that plum eye shadow goes perfectly with your dress."

"Mommeee!" Joey literally squealed the word as he raced down the hall. "There's this gigantic car in front of the house! It's at least a mile long. Come look!"

Kelly and Margie exchanged puzzled glances and followed Joey into the living room.

"Oh, brother!" Margie exclaimed as they peered out the window. "It's a limousine. The man sent a limo for you, Kel." Katie, who had been watching a cartoon on television, hurried over to the window as well.

Samantha giggled. "This is so exciting. Wait till I tell my friends. I'm going to call them right now." She took off in the direction of the telephone.

The doorbell rang. Kelly and Margie backed away from the window, gazing at each other in absolute shock.

"Answer the door, Joey," Margie said. "It's probably the chauffeur."

Kelly grabbed her friend by the wrist. "What'll I do?" she whispered frantically. "I've never ridden in a limo in my life!" Oh, why had Macon done this? she wondered. He probably was trying to make up for not picking her up himself, but she'd feel so awkward riding in such a car. Sadly, she realized how much it emphasized their different lifestyles.

"Stop looking so horrified," Margie said. "You're supposed to be excited. Oh, Kel, please call me from the limo. There'll be a telephone in it, you know."

She was prevented from saying anything else as the front door was thrown open by an excited Joey. A man in a spiffy black suit and cap stepped in. He took off the cap and nodded formally at the group.

"I'm here to pick up Miss Garrett," he said.

Kelly stepped forward. "I'm Kelly Garrett," she said in what she hoped was her most sophisticated voice. "Would you give me just a minute to collect my things? Joey, close the front door so the flies don't come in." She shut her eyes in defeat. That was probably the most unsophisticated thing she'd ever said. Well, too late now, she'd already said it. "Oh, and Joey, please don't ask the man a million questions." She hurried down the hall toward her bedroom with Margie and Katie on her heels.

Joey studied the uniformed man with unveiled

curiosity. "Do you have to pay double when you take that thing to a car wash?" he asked.

Kelly returned a few minutes later, carrying a small clutch bag. "I'm ready," she said breathlessly. The chauffeur nodded and ushered her out the door and to the car. Kelly glanced over her shoulder before she stepped in. Margie and her kids were staring out the window, eyes wide as saucers. The man followed Kelly's gaze and smiled.

Kelly sighed, trying to affect a bored tone. "You'd think by now they'd be used to this sort of thing."

"Yes, ma'am" was all he said before he closed the door to the car, closeting her in the very lap of luxury. She immediately spied the telephone. She had her family on the line before they pulled out of the neighborhood, and spent much of her ride describing the interior of the car to them. She felt like Cinderella and told herself to enjoy it while it lasted. Tomorrow she would be Kelly Garrett again, sweeping cinders from the fireplace. Finally she hung up and placed a quarter beside the telephone to cover the cost of the call.

Kelly knew they had left civilization as she knew it and had entered the filthy-rich district, as she called it. Still, she was not prepared for the sight of the mansion that loomed overhead when the chauffeur helped her out of the car. The house had to have at least thirty rooms, she thought, gazing at the enormous brick structure in absolute wonder. And to think, all she'd ever wanted in life was a four-bedroom house so Samantha and Katie wouldn't have to share a room.

"Are you sure this is the right place?" she asked the chauffeur anxiously.

"Yes, ma'am."

"Oh. Well, perhaps I should just wait in the car until Mr. Bridges arrives." She turned to climb back inside the limo.

"Mr. Bridges specifically requested you meet him inside, madam. I'm sure you'll be more comfortable there."

Kelly seriously doubted it but relented just the same. "Well, uh, thanks for driving me," she said, feeling more flustered by the minute.

The chauffeur bowed low. "My pleasure, madam. Have a nice evening."

Kelly climbed the steps to the house, feeling more self-conscious every moment. She should have stayed home, told Macon if he couldn't pick her up personally, she wouldn't go. But he hadn't even had time to discuss it with her. He'd merely given Samantha the message and hung up.

If Kelly had felt self-conscious before, it was nothing compared to the outright embarrassment she suffered when an austere-looking butler ushered her into the main room of the house. It was filled with men in tuxedos and women in sequined gowns. She wanted to die. An older woman hurried toward her in a shimmering gown of gold lamé. Kelly thought she had never seen anyone move with such grace. The woman seemed to float.

"You must be Miss Garrett," she said, offering a perfectly manicured hand. "I'm Edith Higginbothom. Please call me Edie."

"I'm Kelly." Kelly took her hand and shook it.

"Macon called to say he'd be late," Edie said, smiling sweetly, "and I'm to take care of you until he arrives."

"I'm afraid I'm a bit . . . underdressed," Kelly said, feeling like Beaver Cleaver's mother in her pristine pink dress with its wide peter pan collar. And it had looked so smart in the pattern book. "Macon didn't tell me this was a formal affair." And she would kill him when she saw him, she decided. First, she'd kill him for not coming for her himself, then she'd kill him for letting her show up at this hifalutin party looking like a washwoman. Yes, she'd kill him twice.

"You look absolutely gorgeous," Edie said. "You'll be the belle of the ball." She took Kelly's hand and squeezed it reassuringly. "Now, what would you like to drink?"

"Something laced with cyanide will be fine."

Edie threw back her head and laughed, a delightful, almost musical sound. "Macon didn't tell me what a charming personality you had. And I was so afraid this was going to be another one of those dull evenings. I'm going to go into the dining room before dinner and move the place cards so the two of us can sit close to each other. Now, how about a glass of champagne?" She took a filled glass from a passing waiter's tray and handed it to Kelly. "Come meet everyone, dear." She led Kelly farther into the crowded room. "I'm sure Macon will be here as soon as he can."

Macon arrived only minutes before Edie and

her husband, Max, led their guests into an elaborate dining room. Kelly was so happy and relieved to see him, she forgot about killing him for a moment. Perhaps he hadn't known everyone was going to pull out their finery for the party. He looked wonderful in a black tuxedo and crisp white shirt himself. Tuxedo? So he *had* known it was going to be formal. The worm. She quickly added torture to the list of crimes she planned to commit against his person.

"Why didn't you tell me we were dressing up tonight?" she asked, trying to smile between gritted teeth.

Macon gazed down at her, thinking she had never looked more beautiful. "I was afraid you wouldn't come if I told you. I couldn't get out of coming tonight, and I couldn't stand the thought of not seeing you. I'm sorry for being selfish and insensitive, Kelly, but I knew you would never spend the money on a gown and you'd refuse to let me buy it for you."

His honesty caught her off guard, as well as the genuine remorse in his voice. "Don't be ridiculous," she said, feeling a bit silly for making such a big deal out of it. She tried to appear flippant.

"Kelly, you're the most beautiful woman in the room," he said, his voice little more than a whisper. He felt like a heel for not telling her the party was formal. "You look . . ." He paused, trying to think of the right word, *anything* to make her feel comfortable.

"I look like I should be serving the food instead

of eating it," she said flatly, overcome by another fit of insecurity. "Oh, Macon, I don't have the first thing in common with these people. I come from simple stock, country folk. My parents still live in the farmhouse they bought when they were married. They raised five kids there, and none of us ever really gave much thought to material things. Please don't let me do anything stupid at dinner . . . like wash my hair in the water glass."

"You worry too much," he said, slipping an arm around her waist to escort her to the dining room. "Why should you care what these people think? Oh, here are our seats."

But Kelly *did* care what they thought of her, and she realized over dinner that she was trying to impress Macon's friends much as she'd tried to impress her ex-husband's. She'd obviously failed the first time, because her husband had left her for someone who could do a better job. If she failed Macon, she would never forgive herself.

Thankfully, dinner went without a hitch, and Edie and her husband, as well as Macon, did their best to make her feel at ease. Afterward, Macon took her for a long drive. Eventually, he parked beside a playground and cut the engine.

When he turned to speak to her, he was silent for a moment, distracted by how lovely she looked in the moonlight. "I'm sorry I couldn't pick you up tonight," he said at last. "I did everything in my power to try to speed up the meeting, but I think I was the only one there with plans for the evening."

"That's okay," she mumbled. But it really wasn't.

"I left the meeting long enough to call the limo service for you. I had wanted to send a Rolls Royce, but there was a fancy wedding in town and they were all being used. I wanted to send a white Rolls and a dozen red roses. I called around, but I sort of ran out of time."

"It's okay," she repeated. And this time it was. She could not remember a time when somebody had gone to that much trouble for her.

He took her hand and pressed it to his lips. "There's a fairly good chance I'm going to get to build the convention center in Houston."

"Oh, that's wonderful news. When did you find out?"

"This afternoon. It's not final yet, but rumor has it the architect wants me for the job. I should know for sure next week."

She leaned over and kissed him on the cheek. "Congratulations. I'm very proud of you."

Before she could move away, he grasped her chin with his thumb and forefinger and tilted her head so that she was looking directly into his eyes. "There's only one problem with that, Kelly," he said. "It means I'll be spending a lot of time there in the beginning. I won't see you as much."

"Oh." Her heart sank. "Well, you have to do what you have to do," she said, trying to sound mature about the whole thing but at the same time wondering when and if she would see him.

He brushed his lips gently against hers. "I'll be home on weekends. And I want you to know that when I'm in town, you'll be my top priority. I don't care if everything else comes tumbling down around me, the weekends will be *our* time." With that, he captured her lips again.

All of her doubts faded away in Macon's arms. Kelly thought she had surely died and gone to heaven, so sweet, so wonderful was his mouth on hers. She leaned into the kiss, reveling in the feel of his hard chest, the strong arms that enfolded her. When he broke away, they both gasped for air.

"I'm crazy about you, Kelly," he said simply.

The look on his face almost stole her breath. She wanted to confess her own feelings, but she didn't trust her voice. Instead, she snuggled against him and closed her eyes, content just to be held by him. At the moment nothing else mattered.

Macon leaned down and with every bit of tenderness he could muster, kissed her closed eyelids. Then he kissed her forehead, the tip of her nose, and the tiny cleft in her chin. When he took her mouth again, she was ready for him, and she parted her lips to greet him. It was a long, hungry kiss, filled with an urgency that surprised them both.

"I want to make love to you so bad I hurt," he said, his warm breath fanning her cheek. "Am I moving too fast for you?"

Kelly thought her heart would surely detach itself and take flight, it fluttered so badly. Her voice trembled when she spoke. "Maybe just a little," she finally said. But the truth of the matter was, she *wanted* him to make love to her. She couldn't think of anything she wanted more than to lie in his arms and have him kiss her senseless. But then what? she wondered. Where would they go from there? For she knew that making love with Macon would bind him to her heart forever, and she wasn't certain there was a place for her in his life.

He squeezed her tightly before letting her go. "I'd better take you home, pretty lady," he said. "Before I show you just how fast I *can* move when I'm sorely tempted."

"I'm telling you it's just a simple barbecue with some of the people you met last weekend," Macon said when he called Kelly early the following Saturday. "Max and Edie will be there. You liked them, didn't you?"

Kelly yawned into the telephone. She hadn't been up long. How was she supposed to make snap decisions when she was still half asleep? Macon, she knew, was an early riser. But then, he didn't have trouble with insomnia like she did. "Where's the barbecue going to be?" she asked.

"Close to where you were last week. But everybody will be dressed casually this time, so you don't have to go to a lot of fuss. Just wear jeans or shorts."

Yeah, right, she thought. Those people probably didn't even own a pair of jeans. "What time do you want me to be ready?"

He paused. "Well, I'm supposed to drop by early

to go over a few contracts with some of the people who will be there. You can either come with me, or I'll drive over and pick you up once we're finished."

Kelly told herself she should have known it was business. Although Macon had come by several times during the past week, he was never far from his briefcase or the telephone. She was beginning to think she'd have to have the briefcase surgically removed if they ever decided to become intimate. But the truth was, she wanted to see him, and nothing else really mattered.

"Why don't I just meet you there?" she suggested. "That way I can spend some time with my kids."

After a few minutes of arguing, Macon reluctantly agreed to let her drive herself to the barbecue, and gave her careful directions.

Several hours later Kelly and Margie stood before Kelly's open closet, flipping through the hangers.

"He said it's going to be informal," Kelly said, "but you know what that means. It simply means the women won't be wearing their tiaras."

Margie shot her a speculative glance. "You don't sound happy to be going."

Kelly's expression was grim. "He's way out of my league, Margie." She reminded her friend about the dinner and how she'd been dressed compared to the others. "I was so self-conscious with his friends, I couldn't relax and enjoy myself. I was afraid I'd say or do the wrong thing."

"I thought you said this guy came from humble beginnings."

"He's come a long way since then, believe me." She paused. "I didn't even know what I was eating last week. It was some kind of French food that I couldn't pronounce. At least at a barbecue I should be able to identify the food, huh?"

"You worry too much." Margie pulled out a pants suit. "This is outdated, you need to donate it to the Salvation Army." She tossed it onto the bed and continued to search through the closet.

"And I have absolutely nothing in common with his friends," Kelly continued. "The women talk of flying to Paris for fittings and vacationing in places I've never even heard of. I felt like a first-rate hick. I could never fit into his world."

"Having money doesn't make them better than you, Kel."

Kelly shrugged. "It sort of reminded me of all those times I tried to impress my ex and his friends. Except that Macon doesn't point out all my mistakes at the end of the evening like Bob did."

"You have an inferiority complex, kiddo, you know that? There are times when I'd like to wring your ex-husband's neck for giving it to you."

"It wasn't all his fault. He was just ambitious, and I let him down. I wasn't one for bridge or golf or women's clubs. I preferred thrift shops and flea markets to shopping for designer fashions I couldn't afford in the first place. But why am I telling you this? You've heard it all before."

"Maybe you just needed to talk about it."

Kelly pulled out a black tuxedo-style jump suit from the back of her closet and studied it, then returned it to the rack. "I don't want my children to grow up like their father," she said, thinking out loud. "That's why I'm almost thankful at times that he's too busy to see them often. And I don't like the way he pushes them, as though they aren't doing enough in life. They're just kids."

"Well, I can't say that I blame you for that," Margie said. "But from what you've told me about Bob's own upbringing, it probably has something to do with the way he was raised. He had to go to the best schools and graduate at the top of his class. It wasn't enough that he played football, he had to be the best on the team. Why did you put that jump suit back? Don't you like it?"

Kelly retrieved the jump suit and held it up for a closer look. "Yeah, and now look how he treats his children. It isn't enough that Samantha made the honor role at school this year; he wants to know why she didn't do it all along. And why isn't Joey playing better ball, and how come Katie isn't more advanced in her dance class?" She fingered the material of the garment while she talked. "Don't you think this is too dressy for a barbecue? It's really something you'd want to wear to a nice restaurant. Only I haven't been to a nice restaurant in months, which is when I made this outfit. Lord, I don't even know if it's in style."

Margie studied it. "What else do you have?"

"Nothing. But this material is too . . . rich for day wear."

"Did you say 'rich'?"

Kelly laughed. "You're right. I should fit right in."

When Kelly arrived at the barbecue that afternoon, she discovered, much to her embarrassment, that she was the only one not wearing jeans or shorts. A maid led her around the side of the impressive house to the backyard, a perfect manicured lawn flanked by gardens and enormous hedges. A bright yellow canopy offered relief from the heat, beneath which sat long tables draped in red-and-white checked cloths and adorned with great pots of fresh flowers. A country-western band played from the bricked terrace, and a few couples were doing their best to dance without working up a sweat.

If anyone noticed Kelly was slightly overdressed, they had the good manners not to mention it. Several women made a fuss over her outfit and demanded to know the designer, and there was much to-do when Kelly confessed she'd made it herself. Macon beamed proudly at her side when Edie asked to borrow the pattern.

"Having a good time?" he asked once they'd finished a dinner of barbecued ribs with all the trimmings, and had started on a dessert of home-made butter pecan ice cream.

"I'm having a great time," she said honestly. Except for feeling a little self-conscious about her outfit, she truly was enjoying herself.

"Then how about dancing with me?" he asked as the band struck up a slow number. She nodded and followed him to the terrace, where several other couples had already gathered.

When Kelly stepped into Macon's arms, she felt as though she'd just come home after being away for a long time. It was odd, but nice, like greeting the first spring day after a long and wearisome winter. Like waking to the first rays of sunshine after a lonely, sleepless night.

Snuggling deeper into Macon's arms, she pondered the sensation. She had not realized until that moment how lonely she'd been. The realization jolted her. She had thought her emotional needs were being met by the love of her children. She had thought her life was full. Now she realized that busy and full were not the same thing. Only occasionally had she really missed the company of a man, and she always reminded herself at those times that she had been just as alone during her marriage.

There in Macon's arms, she admitted how much she'd missed being held by a man. More important, she realized she didn't want to be held by just *any* man. She wanted to be held by Macon. She wanted to feel the length of him pressed against her, just as he was now. She wanted to rest her head against his chest and inhale the scent of him and feel his warm breath in her hair. It felt good to be cuddled and cradled and pampered, all those things that came with loving. She had spent so many years nurturing her children, and she loved being on the receiving end at last.

"Is something wrong?" Macon asked, noticing

for the first time how quiet Kelly had become. He'd been so wrapped up in his own thoughts of how good she felt, and the ache that her nearness always aroused, he hadn't noticed her silence.

Kelly met his gaze. The captivating look in his eyes was one of raw need. It shook her right down to her toes. "I was just thinking how nice this is," she said breathlessly. "You and me close together." She inhaled sharply when his hard thighs grazed her own. Every nerve ending in her body seemed to come alive.

"It could be even nicer," he said, and pressed his lips to her forehead. It took every ounce of willpower he had to keep from crushing her in his arms. She was so small, so utterly feminine. Something deep inside of him, some primal urging, he supposed, made him want to take her and make her exclusively his. He wanted to touch the body that so often haunted him in the night and made him gaze off into space during business meetings. He wanted to watch her eyes darken in passion, know the joy of filling her with himself and feel her quiver beneath him. He wanted to hear her soft sigh of contentment. And his male ego assured him he could make her feel all these things.

When he spoke again, his voice was so low, Kelly had to strain to hear him. "Come home with me," he said. "We'll have the place all to ourselves. We can be alone."

She was so surprised with the request, she missed her step and her foot landed solidly on his. Thankfully, he didn't seem to notice. "Yes, Macon," she said, her own voice a mere whisper.

Driving her old Buick, Kelly followed Macon's car to another section of town. The neighborhood was fashionable, some of the houses several stories high and situated on two-acre lots. Macon parked in front of a modern structure of glass and cedar, and she pulled in behind him.

"It's big," she said as he helped her out of her car.

"Yes, it is big," he agreed. "I bought it for entertaining purposes. Want to come in?"

She nodded, and they walked hand in hand to the front door. Macon had to deal with an elaborate security system before they could enter, but finally he led her into an impressive foyer. The house was breathtaking, if not actually homey. Kelly merely stood at the doorway to the living room for a moment, taking it all in, the stark white carpeting, the modern slate-blue sofa and chairs, the glass and chrome end tables. The only bright colors in the room came from massive paintings that adorned the walls, equally modern and dominated by splashes of red and yellow paint.

She didn't quite know what to make of it all.

The kitchen was much the same, she discovered as Macon ushered her into a room that would have swallowed her entire house whole. The appliances were clean and white and shone like a new Cadillac. The floor was solid slate and, Kelly decided, must have cost a fortune. It was a kitchen one would expect to find in *Architectural Digest*.

"I'm impressed," she finally said.

"It's okay, but it's not cozy like your place." He glanced around the room and shrugged. "It serves its purpose, and I get a good tax writeoff, so what the hell. Come on, I'll show you my room."

"You say there's nobody else here?" she asked, glancing around the room as though half expecting someone to come through the door.

"I have a live-in housekeeper, but she's out."

Kelly nodded and followed him back into the foyer and up a staircase to the second floor, where his master suite was located. Although the modern decor had been maintained in his bedroom, it was somewhat softened by draperies and books and personal belongings. A quick glance into the bathroom showed her a massive Jacuzzi surrounded by mirrors. And finally, when she could no longer ignore it, she was forced to acknowledge the king-size bed, perched on a chrome frame and draped in a satin slate-blue coverlet.

Macon's gaze never left her face as she walked about the room, touching a vase, running her fingers lightly over a masculine jewelry box. Her smile, when she faced him, was tremulous.

"I'm nervous," she confessed. "Does it show?"

He felt his heart turn over in his chest. He was reminded once again of a young girl, a bit shy, and very unsure of herself at the moment. He closed the distance between them and folded her in his arms. "Would you rather not stay?" he asked. For him, it was the supreme sacrifice. He wanted her desperately, with every fiber of his being, but he wanted her to feel good about it.

"I have to tell you something," she whispered. She glanced away from him and laughed self-consciously. "No, don't look at me or I'll never get through it."

"I'm listening."

"I haven't been with many men, Macon. I could probably count them all on one finger. At times I wanted to, but the opportunity never presented itself." She realized she was talking very quickly. "Things never progressed to that stage."

She was fidgeting with her hands, and he took them in his own to still them. "Why are you telling me this?"

She frowned. "I'm afraid I'll disappoint you. I don't have a gorgeous body like most women you probably go out with. I have . . . imperfections."

He seemed to consider that, though amusement sparkled in his eyes. "You don't have a bunch of tattoos on your body, do you?" he finally asked.

She laughed in spite of her nervousness. "No, it's nothing like that."

He made a production of looking relieved. "Thank goodness. I can handle anything but tattoos." Then, smiling gently, he pulled her against him. "Go easy on yourself, Kelly," he said, cradling the back of her head in his palm as she gazed up at him. "Everybody has imperfections. That's the beauty of being human." He grinned suddenly. "But if it'll make you feel better, I'll let you see the scar from my appendectomy."

She laughed softly. "That's okay. But I feel better knowing you have one."

He kissed her tenderly, then walked around the room pulling the drapes, locking out the late afternoon sun. She loved him more for it.

When he was through he took her in his arms again and held her for a long moment. She shivered, and he tightened his hold on her. "What do you want me to do, Kelly? Just tell me."

"I want you to make love to me," she said breathlessly, knowing in her heart she belonged to him. At that moment it didn't matter who or where they were, only that she cared deeply for him, possibly loved him, and wanted to know him in the most intimate way.

Without having to be told twice, Macon swept her into his arms and carried her to the bed. He was reminded once again of her size and smiled down at her. "You're no bigger than a minute," he said. The smile she returned made his heart beat faster. Her eyes shone like burnished copper. He lowered her gently onto the mattress, taking a moment to remove her shoes and massage her feet. They were so amazingly dainty.

"While we're confessing all our insecurities," he said, "maybe I should tell you how oafish I sometimes feel next to you. You're so tiny and graceful, and I feel like the bull in the china shop."

His confession touched her. "You're the most handsome man in the world," she said. "Not to mention the sexiest." She slid her arms around his neck. "You wouldn't believe the fantasies I've had about you."

His eyebrows arched in surprise, but his eyes gleamed with pleasure. "Really?"

She nodded. "I think of how you'd look in the shower," she admitted as her cheeks flushed. Along with the strong sensual threads that bound them together, she knew there was also an underlying sense of trust and friendship and acceptance. "Why do you think I spend half the night wallpapering my bathroom and moving furniture?"

He raised her hand to his lips and kissed her palm. "I'm glad you told me that. As for myself, you should see the nicks I've given myself shaving, just because I can't get you off my mind. I finally bought an electric shaver."

Laughter bubbled from Kelly's throat as she reached up and slowly unbuttoned his shirt, forcing herself to take the initiative. Surprisingly, her desire to touch him thoroughly quelled her inhibitions. Her gaze locked with his. "Do you mind?"

He shook his head. "Not in the least."

She sat up and pulled his shirttail free, laying the shirt open and exposing the most beautiful chest she'd ever seen. She plunged her fingers into the crisp black hair, letting the curls slip around her fingers like silken rings. His muscles flexed in response, and he closed his eyes, as though branding the memory of her touch in his mind.

Kelly toyed with the curls for a moment, trailing her fingers to where they thinned out over his flat stomach and whorled around his navel in a most fascinating manner. His nipples were brown and nubby, and they puckered the instant she touched them. Without stopping to think, she leaned forward and brushed one with her lips, then licked it with the tip of her tongue. The husky moan from Macon's throat prodded her onward.

A half smile playing on her lips, she swirled her tongue around his nipple, then caught it between her teeth. She nipped it, soothed it with her tongue, and nipped it again, delighting in the goose pimples on his shoulders. It was a heady, exhilarating feeling to know that she had this much power over such a self-assured man. It gave her a feeling of control, an emotion that was quite new to her, especially where Macon was concerned.

He smiled down at her lazily, his lids heavy, his eyes smoky with desire. "You're a witch, Kelly Garrett."

She laughed. She felt beautiful and desirable. The look in Macon's eyes proved it. She suddenly wanted to embrace the world. "And you're putty in my hands, Macon Bridges," she teased.

"Oh, yeah?" This seemed to amuse him greatly. He peeled off his shirt and tossed it aside, then, without warning, grasped both her wrists and pushed her back on the bed, raising himself over her and wedging a knee between her thighs. "We'll see about that."

She was still smiling when his mouth opened over hers. His tongue searched out all her hidden places, giving her own tongue a run for its money. A knot of tension tightened in the pit of her stomach while his knee made a gentle sawing motion between her thighs. It was enough to drive her over the edge.

He broke the kiss, but his lips reappeared at the base of her throat and again at her earlobe, tasting and sampling the textures that awaited him. He eased her up long enough to unzip her jump suit, and in a matter of seconds pulled the garment away, leaving her in her bra and panties.

He sprang off the bed, draping her outfit over a chair and then undressing. As he worked at the fastening of his jeans, he never took his gaze off her face. He stepped out of the jeans and they joined her jump suit on the chair. His briefs quickly followed the same route.

Kelly gazed at him with feminine appreciation. Even in the dim light she could pick out the perfect lines of his body. He was a big man, but not burly or clumsy-looking. His legs were long and lean and muscular. Although she had seen him in his bathing suit, it was not the same as viewing him totally naked. She followed his legs upward to where a thatch of black curls nestled around his swollen sex. He walked toward her. He was a beautiful man, she decided.

"I don't see your scar," she said. At his blank expression, she added, "From when you had your appendix removed."

He gave an embarrassed cough, but amusement lurked in his eyes. "I'm afraid I . . . uh, lied about that. I thought it would help you relax. But I have a nasty gash on the heel of my foot where I once stepped on a piece of glass."

She shot him an indignant look. "You lied to me," she said, pointing an accusing finger at him.

Her lips twitched at the corners, and it was all she could do to keep from laughing as he attempted to appear remorseful. She grabbed a pillow and threw it at him as hard as she could, but he ducked. "I'll get you back for that one of these days, Macon Bridges."

Laughing, he strode to the bed and recaptured her lips before she could slip away. Their playful mood turned serious, and he removed the rest of her clothes. When she lay naked before him, he gazed down at her with love and adoration. "Don't ever try to convince me you're anything less than perfect," he said. And suddenly, his lips were everywhere.

Kelly's world became a place of sensations as Macon's mouth traveled lovingly over her body, wreaking havoc with her nervous system. He kissed her breasts until her nipples hardened in anticipation. His hands never stilled, stroking and teasing her until she thought she'd go into a fit. It was as though a fog had settled around her brain, because all rational thinking ceased. Every time she tried to pull her thoughts together, his lips dragged her deeper into the cloud.

And then his mouth skimmed across her belly to her thighs, caressing them playfully before feasting on what lay between. It was Kelly's undoing. She squeezed her eyes closed as his tongue explored her, stripping her bare so there were no longer any secrets between them. A wave of sheer delight washed over her, followed by another, stronger and more intense than the first.

Macon raised up and, sweeping her legs farther apart, entered her cautiously. Their sighs of pleasure rose like music over their heads. He moved against her, catching her up swiftly in his erotic dance. Their movements quickened with each heartbeat, and the frenzied finale made them cry out. The sound was stifled with the meeting of lips. Macon shuddered against her as the last note tore from his body.

They were totally spent. Macon rolled off her and gathered her into his arms, where she snuggled against him like a soft kitten.

Kelly reveled in the languor, using the quiet time to reflect on her feelings for the man beside her. Her hand on his chest measured the steady rhythm of his heart, and she listened as his breathing slowed. His masculine scent enveloped her, making her giddy. She was smiling, grinning from ear to ear, actually, drunk on happiness. She felt treasured in his arms, priceless. Special. For the first time in her life, she believed there wasn't anything she couldn't do.

She hitched herself up on one elbow and gazed down at him lovingly. His smile was lazy, satisfied. He winked at her. Such a small gesture, but it conveyed so much. He was pleased with her. At that moment she felt pretty pleased with herself. She lowered her head and kissed him, her hair grazing his shoulder. He ran his big hands along her back and cupped one hip in his palm, squeezing it playfully. And when they began to make love again, Kelly was just as happy as before, just as greedy for him.

In his arms she became beautiful and precious, and when they climaxed together, their very souls joined. She loved him with all her heart, she realized. This was the stuff that poets spun sonnets over, the kind of loving that inspired love songs. But there was more to it than that. With Macon she was beginning to love herself. And of all his gifts, she treasured that most.

It was still early in the evening when he walked her to her car and watched her drive off after a long, lingering kiss and a promise to call the following day. He had wanted her to stay, but he knew she wanted to spend time with her children. He returned to his empty house and worked until he fell asleep.

Kelly tossed in her bed that night for close to an hour thinking of Macon. They had made love. She still couldn't believe it. The scent of his aftershave lingered with her, on her body, in her hair. The feel of his lips was fresh in her mind, as was the rapturous look on his face when he'd taken her. That look had said it all.

She was head over heels in love with Macon Bridges, and it scared the daylights out of her.

Kelly was up in an instant, groping in the dark for the bathroom door. She found it, flipped on the light, and sighed at the sight of her half-papered bathroom. Then she went to work.

Five

Kelly found no clean clothes the following morning, so she didn't bother waking her children for church.

Margie, on her way to the airport to pick up her son, who'd been visiting his father over the summer, dropped by for a cup of coffee. "You look exhausted," she told Kelly. "You must've finished wallpapering your bathroom last night."

Kelly nodded. "I should have washed clothes instead," she said, still feeling pretty guilty that her children weren't in church. She couldn't remember ever missing Sunday school as a child. "I didn't realize I was so far behind on everything."

"It's your love life," Margie teased. "Which reminds me, how'd it go yesterday?"

Before Kelly could say anything, a hot blush

spread across her face to the tops of her ears. "Uh, fine," she finally managed.

"That good, huh?" Margie burst into hearty laughter and she slapped her friend on the back. Kelly glared at her. "I was beginning to think you weren't normal like the rest of us, girl." She sobered abruptly. "Are you in love with him?"

Kelly sighed. "It has to be love. I can't explain any other reason for feeling this way. I'm shaky, my heart races all the time, and I can't lie still at night. And when I think about him, I break out in a cold sweat. Then, all of a sudden I get this hot flush over my whole body."

"Might be the flu." Margie reached over and placed her hand against Kelly's forehead.

Kelly chuckled. "Believe me, it would be much easier putting up with the flu."

"Oh, yes, I can see where it would be more fun lying in bed sick than going out with a wealthy, good-looking man who is crazy about you."

Kelly wasn't listening. "What makes you think Macon would be any different from Bob?" she asked, thinking out loud. "I mean, can you see a man like Macon sitting down to dinner every night with a family, or playing ball with his children in the backyard? He has his own private jet, for Pete's sake."

Margie screwed up her face in thought. "I'm not sure what the jet has to do with this conversation, but, no, I can't see him playing ball in the backyard. He can afford to pay someone to do it for him," she added laughingly, then paused when

Kelly continued to look worried. "What are you going to do?"

Kelly shook her head. "I don't know. I need time to think. Things are moving too fast for me. I haven't known him long, and look how far things have progressed. I've lost control. Common sense just flies out the window when he touches me. I'm scared to death, Margie."

"Are you planning to see him today?"

"He said he'd call. But I'm going to tell him I've got too much to do. Which is the truth. Maybe if Macon realizes I can't just drop everything and be there for him whenever he calls, he'll back off."

"Is that what you want?" Margie asked softly.

"I don't know *what* I want," Kelly confessed. "But I can't always be accessible to Macon, and the sooner he realizes it, the better off we'll be. I have three children and a career and a house to care for." She sighed and covered her face with her hands. "I knew from the beginning it was a mistake to get involved with him, but I couldn't help it. I knew we were too different, and that I'd end up paying dearly if I became emotionally entangled, but . . ." She dropped her hands and stared at her friend. "I found out last night it was too late to worry about it anymore. All this time, I've been talking to myself and warning myself about what could happen, and somewhere along the way I fell in love with him anyway."

Macon called an hour later. Kelly got goose pimples at the sound of his husky voice. "I miss you," he said without preamble, and his words seemed to caress her as his lips had the night before. "Why don't you and the kids come over today? We could cook out and swim in the pool."

It sounded wonderful. She was on the verge of accepting but stopped herself. "Macon, I'd love to, but I can't."

"Don't you want to see me, honey?"

"Of course, but I have a ton of work to do around here," she said, standing firm despite his obvious disappointment. "The house is a mess, and the laundry is piled to the ceiling. And I have all this . . . uh, yard work to do. My flower beds are filled with weeds, and the dandelions are taking over, and the grass is ankle-deep."

"Good grief!"

"Yes, well, I don't really have time to do everything during the week, so I have to catch up on the weekends. But thanks for calling just the same. 'Bye now." She hung up the phone before he could say anything else. "Well, that's that," she said, then hurried to her room to change clothes. Perhaps Macon would realize she didn't live a fairy-tale existence like his friends, and that she had responsibilities and obligations.

Coward, she chided herself mentally. Her refusal to see him had nothing to do with the chores that waited for her. She was running scared and she knew it. Every time she laid eyes on the man, her feelings for him strengthened. She had to back off, get a perspective on the situation. Common sense told her nothing could come of the relationship, and no amount of wishing and hoping was going to change it. Macon Bridges was a workaholic who lived in the fast lane, and while she might serve as a momentary diversion, there was no place in his life for a woman with three children. Now, how many times was she going to have to remind herself of those facts?

Shortly after lunch Kelly spied two uniformed men kneeling in her front yard, staring at her dandelions as though they hoped to uncover some dark secret as to their origin. She dropped her basket of clean laundry and threw open the front door.

"What do you think you're doing?" she demanded. Katie and Joey scampered up behind her, poking their heads around her to see what was going on.

One of the men stood and tipped his cap back. "Afternoon, ma'am. We're trying to figure out how to kill off all these dandelions. I reckon this is about as bad as it gets, know what I mean?" He chuckled. "I reckon you could say you've been blessed in the dandelion department."

Kelly stared at him in bafflement, then noticed the white van parked in her driveway. The logo painted on the side identified them as a lawn and garden service.

"I didn't hire your service," she said quickly, stepping onto the front porch and planting her hands on her hips. "And don't you dare kill one dandelion, because I can't afford to pay you."

"The bill has already been taken care of, ma'am," he said. "Mr. Bridges—"

"What about Mr. Bridges?"

"He sent us over."

She crossed her arms. Macon Bridges had some nerve. Was this his way of showing appreciation for the night before? "Well, you can just tell Mr. Bridges that I don't need his charity. I can take care of my own yard, thank you very much."

The man looked doubtful. "These are pretty tough dandelions, ma'am. They ain't going to be easy to kill."

"I don't care if I have to hire Freddy Kreuger for the job," she said, "but you aren't going to do it." She slammed the door, whipped around and ran smack into Samantha.

"What in the world are you so mad about?" the girl demanded. "I'm sure Macon was only trying to help. You didn't have to yell at those men like that."

Kelly found all three of her children watching her warily. She plodded into the den and sank onto the couch. They followed. "I guess I got carried away, huh?"

"You might say that," Samantha agreed.

Kelly buried her face in her hands. "I'm just so tired. I never sleep anymore. All I do is hang wallpaper and clean out closets and cabinets."

Samantha gave her mother a sympathetic look. "Why don't you take a nap, Mom?" she said, reaching for a throw pillow. "I'll fold the laundry while you rest. And don't worry about Joey or Katie. They can play in the backyard."

Kelly shook her head when Samantha knelt before her and quickly untied the laces on her sneakers. "I'll never be able to sleep," she grumbled. "I'm just too wound up. Too much on my mind, I guess." Boy, falling in love was really rough on the system, she thought. She lay back on the couch, adjusting the pillow so that it was comfortable. "I might just rest my eyes for a minute." She was vaguely aware of Samantha ushering Katie and Joey out of the room and closing the door softly behind them. Then she slept.

When Kelly opened her eyes, she felt as though she had slept a long time. She was calm and rested, and that made her smile. She lay there a moment, listening to the steady hum of the lawn mower coming from the back yard. Sitting up, she stretched. Samantha must have decided to mow the grass for her.

But Kelly found Samantha folding laundry at the kitchen table. "Did you have a nice rest?" Samantha asked. "I washed another load of clothes while you were asleep. Would you like a glass of iced tea?"

"Samantha, who's mowing the grass?" Kelly asked, already hurrying to the kitchen window to look out. She couldn't see anything. "Not Joey, I hope."

"No, Joey and Katie are cleaning their rooms. Macon said he'd take us swimming at his place if we'd straighten the house."

"Macon?"

Samantha nodded. "That's who's mowing the yard. He said he'd mow the front after you woke up from your nap 'cause he didn't want to make noise. And I helped him pull the weeds from the flower beds."

Kelly couldn't take it all in. "Macon is mowing our backyard?" she said in disbelief. She pulled open the sliding glass door and stepped outside just as Macon rounded the corner of the house. He spotted her and waved.

"What are you doing?" she shouted, trying to be heard over the roar of the mower.

He cupped his hand to his ear. "Can't hear you." Instead of stopping to talk, though, he went on.

The sun was blinding. It had to be close to one hundred degrees, Kelly thought. How could he stand it? "Macon, turn that thing off and come inside," she said, running up behind him. She even tugged the back of his shirt, but he ignored her. "Macon!"

"I can't hear you," he repeated, and kept going.

She threw up her hands and stalked toward the house. "That man is impossible," she muttered. When she reentered the kitchen, she found Katie and Joey wearing their bathing suits.

"I finished cleaning my room," Joey announced. "Can we go swimming now? Macon said—"

"I know what Macon said," Kelly told him, "but he didn't bother to clear it with me first." She crossed her arms and tapped her foot impatiently as she heard the mower move in the direction of the front yard. The man really had gall, showing up in her life and making decisions . . . and mowing her grass like . . . like it was *his* grass.

By the time Macon finished mowing the front yard, Kelly, with the help of Samantha, had vacuumed and dusted the house and put fresh linens on the beds. She was just finishing up in the kitchen when he came in, searching for something cold to drink.

She faced him, and her mouth went dry at the sight of his naked chest. He had obviously stripped off his shirt due to the heat, and the black, sweat-glistened curls reminded her of the previous afternoon. She couldn't meet his gaze despite her best efforts.

"Hi." He said the word simply enough, but there was an underlying intimacy in his tone. His gaze dropped to her lips.

It was impossible to be annoyed for very long with a man who looked like that, Kelly decided. His cutoffs were faded and frayed, showing off his tanned and lean legs to advantage. His Reeboks were filthy, edged with grass stains.

"Hi, yourself," she said, pursing her lips to keep from smiling. "What do you mean, barging into my house and ordering everybody around like you own the place? And what gives you the right to tell my children they're going swimming after I said no? And what makes you think I can't take care of my own yard work? I've been doing it for years now."

This seemed to amuse him. His eyes were bright with silent laughter as he stepped closer. "Samantha said you were in a bad mood. I would have thought after last night you'd be . . . less tense."

Her face flamed. "You're changing the subject."

He closed the distance between them and slipped his arms around her waist. "I wanted to see you," he said, leaning his head forward so that his nose touched hers, "and I would have mowed a ten-acre pasture if it meant us spending time together."

The scent of sweat and aftershave left her weak-kneed and trembling. Her nerves were tight as guitar strings, and her heart thumped wildly. "That's . . . no . . . excuse," she finally managed.

He chuckled, and gently kissed her. When he raised his head, he was smiling. "Why don't you let me help you?" he asked. "If you had a house-keeper and a yard man, you wouldn't have all this work to do, and we could spend more time together."

"I can't afford it."

"I can."

She slipped from his grasp and strode to the other side of the kitchen. "Thanks for the offer, but I'm afraid I'll have to pass. Besides, I told you my life-style would drive you crazy, Macon. When I'm not working, I'm trying to make dentist and doctor appointments, or driving my kids to some event, or going to the grocery store, or helping with homework." She sighed. "Weekends aren't much better, I'm afraid. But I can't very well ig-nore my obligations simply because you want me to."

"I know that. But am I out of line to want to see you when I can? You know what my own life is like. I'm seldom in town, and when I am, I'm so caught up in meetings that I can't see straight. Is it so difficult to understand that I want to be with you whenever humanly possible?"

"No, what's hard to understand is why you don't rearrange your own schedule. Don't expect me to make all the sacrifices, Macon. After all, I feel raising my children is just as important as your running a company."

There, she'd said it. Kelly silently congratulated herself. Of course, there was nothing to stop Macon from walking out the door and never coming back, but she would have hated herself had she not told him what was bothering her. And she would grow to resent Macon for not being sensitive to her needs, just as she'd resented Bob. One thing she had learned the past few years was that you had to *ask* for what you wanted. You couldn't expect people to read your mind.

Macon gazed at her thoughtfully. After a moment a smile started at the corners of his lips and spread across his face. "Well, I guess you put me in my place, didn't you?"

The smile was infectious, and before she knew it Kelly found herself grinning. "Yeah, I guess I did."

"You're right, though." He grasped her shoulders and hugged her affectionately. "I shouldn't expect you to arrange your life according to mine. No man should. I guess I've just been doing my own thing for so long that I don't know any other way. But I'll try." He grinned. "Now, would you give me something cold to drink or do I have to drive to the nearest convenience store?"

Kelly nodded and turned to the refrigerator. It had been easier to get what she wanted than she'd thought. Perhaps she should have started long ago.

Joey appeared in the doorway while she was preparing a glass of iced tea for Macon. He looked from one to the other. "Samantha and Katie sent me in here to find out if we're still going swimming?"

"It's up to your mother," Macon said dutifully. When Kelly didn't answer right away, he went on. "I agree that we've all worked hard and deserve a rest, but your mother runs this house . . . and does a darn good job of it if you ask me. It's up to her."

Kelly handed him his glass of tea. "Spreading it on a bit thick, aren't we?" She turned to her son. "Yes, we can go swimming now if Macon still wants us." Joey was out the door before she could finish her sentence, announcing her decision to his sisters.

Macon's pool area was beautifully landscaped and looked more like a remote vacation spot than a backyard. The kidney-shaped pool was surrounded by modern chaise longues and tables, and off to the side sat a wet bar beneath a small striped cabana. It was the perfect spot for entertaining, Kelly decided at once, but she wasn't sure the guest list should include her three children.

Samantha and Joey looked at each other. "Awesome!" they chimed simultaneously.

Kelly thought it the perfect word. "Macon, are you sure you want us—"

"Last one in the pool is a rotten egg!" he shouted, cutting her off, and before Kelly could say another word, all three children had stripped off their outer clothes and dove in. Macon reached for her hand and squeezed it. "I knew they'd like it."

"What's not to like?" she said. "It looks like Palm Springs."

"Why don't you sit down, and I'll ask Mrs. Baxter to make us something cold."

"Mrs. Baxter?"

"My housekeeper. Do you like piña coladas?"

"I love them."

"Great. Take off your wrap and get some sun while it lasts." He strode away to a set of rock steps that led to a patio at the back of the house.

Kelly was beside the pool instantly, motioning for Samantha and Joey to join her at the shallow end, where Katie was playing. "Okay, let's set the ground rules right now," she said. "I don't want any dunking or splashing or running around the pool. And don't get the furniture wet." She started back to her seat, then stopped. "And no yelling, okay?" Her children merely stared back at her in silence.

Kelly didn't hear Macon come up behind her until he let out a sudden shout, grabbed her, and jumped into the water. She screamed loudly before going under.

When she came up coughing and sputtering, Samantha and Joey were waiting with arms folded over their chests.

"I thought you said we weren't supposed to run or splash, Mom," Samantha said.

"Or yell," Joey added.

Macon shook his head, sending water flying from his wet hair. "Who says you can't do all those things?" he asked, his gaze colliding with Kelly's.

"Mom is afraid we'll annoy you," Samantha told him.

Kelly smiled weakly. "They tend to get carried away at times."

"Let them."

Katie edged closer to Macon. "If we annoy you, will you never invite us back? Mommy says if we don't use our manners, people won't want us around."

Macon smiled and reached for the girl, and she straddled his waist with her chubby legs. "You guys are always welcome here, and I don't care how much you yell or splash." He glanced at Kelly. "Your mother is right to teach you manners, though," he added. "Some folks don't like a lot of noise." He began to tickle Katie and threatened to dunk her, to which she responded with squeals and giggles of protest. "But I love noise!" he shouted at the top of his lungs as Samantha and Joey jumped him from both sides, pretending to rescue their sister.

A few minutes later Mrs. Baxter, a large woman

wearing a simple housedress and white apron, carried out a tray of snacks and cold drinks. Macon made introductions as the woman handed Kelly a tall glass filled with frozen piña colada, a slice of fresh pineapple on the rim.

"You won't find anything tastier this side of Puerto Rico," Macon said proudly. "Try it."

"You must be special company," the housekeeper said, smiling warmly at Kelly. "Mr. Bridges has me make these up only for important guests." She indicated the glass.

Kelly tasted her drink. "It's delicious, Mrs. Baxter. Thank you. This is a real treat for me."

The woman glowed under Kelly's praise. "And I have colas for the children. And snacks. Children get so hungry when they play." She glanced at Macon. "You'll call me if you need something?"

Macon nodded and toasted Kelly with his glass as the woman returned to the house. "Glad you came now?" he asked her.

Kelly smiled. "Yes. The kids are having a wonderful time."

"What about you? Are you having a good time?"

"You know I am."

He grinned. "And when you go back home you can rest. All the work has been done, thanks to our great team effort."

She set down her glass. "You probably think my responsibilities are no big deal compared to yours."

"I never said that. In fact, I don't know how you do it. You deserve a lot of credit." When she didn't answer right away, he went on. "But something tells me you aren't used to getting much credit for what you do."

She shrugged. "I'm not so different from a lot of women, I guess. But you're right, I never got much credit for what I did." She was quiet for a moment, remembering. "After Samantha and Joey were born, I wanted to work, at least part-time, because I felt cut off from the rest of the world. My children were my only source of companionship. I didn't go back to work full-time until Joey was almost ready for nursery school. Then I learned I was pregnant with Katie." She shook her head, her expression almost grim.

"You don't sound very happy about that."

Kelly gazed out at her youngest with a soft smile on her face. "Oh, I was thrilled when I had her. She has been a delight. But when I first found out about it, I was devastated. I thought my life was over. Before that time I'd always wanted a big family, like the family I grew up in. But my father played a big part in our lives. My own children didn't have that advantage. In fact, I felt like a single parent most of the time." She shrugged. "I should have put my foot down, forced their father to become more involved."

"Why didn't you?"

"I don't know. I guess I was always intimidated by him. My own husband, can you believe it? He was an honors graduate in college, not to mention a football hero. Later he became a bigshot executive. I felt my needs, and those of my children, weren't as important. His professional life had top priority. He was top dog at work, so it was no wonder he didn't want to do the menial tasks at home like change diapers or bathe his children. It was below him. In the beginning I tried to fight it, but it took a lot out of me. I learned it was easier to go along with everything. But after you live with someone like that for a while, you start feeling like a second-class citizen."

"Why did you stay married to him?"

She picked up her glass and sipped the frozen concoction, taking so long in answering that Macon thought she wasn't going to. "I didn't think I could make it on my own," she said eventually. "And he wasn't a cruel person. That would have made it easier to walk out. He was a good provider, and he was decent to us." She smiled bitterly. "So he made it easy by leaving me."

She turned her head to gaze at her children. "I guess the reason I'm telling you this is to make you understand why I'm a bit pigheaded at times. I don't ever want to feel like a second-class citizen again, and I don't want my children to feel that way either. You can't just put your children on a shelf and take them down when it's convenient. A parent has to be available all the time."

"Do they see their father often?"

"Here and there. Not often, no. And as selfish as it sounds, I don't care. They're not comfortable in his home or around his new wife."

"I envy you," Macon said after a moment.

She laughed. "Me? Why should you of all people envy me? Look at yourself. You know what you want out of life. I've never felt sure of myself like you do. You set your mind on what you wanted to accomplish, and you did it. And you envy me?"

"But look what I gave up. In fact, I sound a lot like your ex-husband."

Kelly turned to him, but was prevented from answering by the sudden appearance of her eldest, who informed her mother she was starving and proceeded to dive into the snacks. Kelly was still pondering his words when Joey and Katie joined them, and she couldn't help but wonder how close to the truth he'd come.

Six

Kelly felt very much at home with Macon, cooking hamburgers and corn on the cob on his grill, and was chatting with him about work as Joey and Katie sat on the edge of the pool, dangling their feet in the water. Samantha had discovered a portable telephone and sat at the far end of the pool, talking into it animatedly. Kelly wondered if she was describing Macon's house to one of her friends.

Macon had given them a brief tour of the place, which included a peek at his game room on the third floor. He'd promised to let Mrs. Baxter, who he claimed was an excellent pool player, teach them to shoot. Kelly got the impression Mrs. Baxter was more than just a housekeeper, and she was thankful Macon had a friend in her. Samantha and Joey had been very impressed with the house, while Katie had shown more interest in the intercom system. Before long, she had loud music blaring into all the rooms. What seemed to strike Samantha the most was the fact that every room, including each bathroom, possessed a telephone. In the meantime Mrs. Baxter had prepared a tossed salad and an impressive relish tray filled with a variety of cheeses and vegetables, which she declared were fresh from her sister's garden. Kelly carried out what they would need for the picnic while Mrs. Baxter finished up in the kitchen.

Dinner was excellent, although Kelly found it difficult to concentrate on her food. She watched her children, wishing they didn't have to look so happy to be with Macon and he with them. Weren't children supposed to be jealous of the new man in their mother's life? And wasn't Macon supposed to resent the time and energy she was forced to devote to them? Instead, he'd spent the morning helping with her chores so they could relax together the rest of the day. It was perfect. They belonged on a breakfast commercial, she thought, one big happy family. But there was only one problem. This scene had absolutely no place in Macon's life.

Kelly simply couldn't figure him out. On one hand, he was the powerful executive, wearing six-hundred-dollar suits, climbing in and out of limos, and jetting all over the country. On the other hand, there he was, wearing the tackiest pair of cutoffs she'd ever laid eyes on and threatening to fire Mrs. Baxter if she threw away his pathetic-looking Reeboks; or he was wrapping up the leftovers in case someone wanted a snack later. The man was an enigma, a contradiction unto himself.

Once dinner was over, she and Macon carried the food and dirty dishes in while Mrs. Baxter ushered the children upstairs for a game of pool. Macon sneaked up behind Kelly while she was rinsing the plates and slipped his arm around her waist. He nuzzled his face against the nape of her neck, sending a delicious shiver up her spine.

"I talked Mrs. Baxter into taking the kids to a movie tonight," he said. "What have you got to say to that?"

She shook her head. "Poor Mrs. Baxter."

He chuckled. "Don't worry, she loves kids. And I think letting her have a couple of days off to visit her sister clinched the deal." He turned her around so that she was looking at him. "Only problem is, I don't know how we'll entertain ourselves while they're gone."

Kelly nodded in agreement. "It will be kind of dull, all that peace and quiet. Maybe we should take a nap."

"Now, why didn't I think of that?"

It wasn't much later when Mrs. Baxter, having piled the kids into her station wagon, pulled out of the driveway with no time to spare to make a nine o'clock movie.

'Katie will never be able to stay awake," Kelly informed Macon.

He grinned. "It doesn't matter. Mrs. Baxter knows she won't get her days off if she brings them home early."

Kelly laughed and slapped him playfully. "You're a vile man, Macon Bridges."

Without warning he grabbed her and swept her up into his arms. "And you're a pipsqueak, Kelly Garrett, and no match for the likes of me. And to prove it, I'm going to whisk you away to my lair and have my way with you."

Hearty laughter bubbled up from her throat, and she clung to his neck as he ran up the stairs with her. She shrieked when he pretended to trip on the last step.

"Boy, you sure make a lot of noise for a lady your size," he teased. "You're going to scare my neighbors."

They were still laughing when they fell unceremoniously onto his bed, but Kelly's smile faded as his mouth opened over hers in a wonderfully heated kiss. For a long moment they merely clung together, sampling each other's mouths. Macon took her bottom lip between his teeth and nibbled on it while his hands ducked under her blouse and cupped her breasts.

"I've been wanting to do this all evening," he confessed in a throaty whisper.

She felt her nipples contract as the heat from his palms seeped through the gauzy fabric of her bra. "Thank you for waiting until my children were gone."

"Good ol' Mrs. Baxter. I may send her on a two-week Caribbean cruise for this."

He captured her lips again in a kiss that left her trembling from head to foot. After hastily removing her clothes, he shrugged off his own. He kissed her all over, worshipping every curve and crevice, all the warm, hidden places. He drew lazy circles around her navel, then dropped to her thighs, where he took delightful love bites. Finally he plunged his tongue into the very heart of her passion. Kelly arched against him and closed her eyes as a violent wave of desire coursed through her, leaving her weak and shaky.

When Macon made a move to enter her, she pushed him aside and, much to his surprise, pleasured him as he had done to her. Finally, with a groan, he rolled her over and sank into her. His mouth covered hers again, his tongue seeking hers as he thrust against her. They climaxed together, and Macon ground his hips against her one final time before shuddering in her arms.

Afterward, they lay side by side, fingers linked, staring up at the ceiling. From time to time they glanced at each other, both wearing a look of total satisfaction.

"Am I smiling real big?" Kelly asked. "My cheeks feel sore, so I must be."

Macon chuckled and pulled her into his arms. Her skin was as smooth as the satin lining of his suits, and he smiled as he realized those expensive suits would now always remind him of her. "If you were smiling any bigger, we'd have to buy you an extra face to fit it on."

She giggled. "You make me feel eighteen again, Rambo."

He arched a brow. "Rambo?"

"Uh-huh." She stretched lazily. "It just seems fitting somehow."

"Please don't call me that in front of Samantha or Mrs. Baxter. They might get suspicious."

"Macon?"

"Hmmm?"

"I think I'm falling in love with you."

He went very still, but inside he was certain his heart had just landed somewhere in his throat. He rose up on one elbow and gazed down at her. "Are you sure?" It was vitally important that she be very sure about what she was saying.

"I know it must be love," she said. "I have this terrible case of insomnia, and when I think of you my heart races, and I get hot and cold at the same time."

He frowned in concern. "I hope you haven't picked up a bug."

She rolled her eyes. "You sound like Margie. I'm telling you, I've never felt like this before."

"Never?"

She met his gaze solemnly. "Never. It's kind of scary."

"Well, I've loved you for some time now," he said, then smiled at her look of surprise. He kissed her tenderly but deeply, trying to pour all of his emotions into that one act. When he lifted his head, his expression was thoughtful. "What are we going to do about it?"

She sighed heavily. "I don't know. I think that's where the insomnia comes in. I spend every waking moment wondering where all this is leading."

She stopped, wondering if she'd said too much. Perhaps he'd think she was trying to pressure him, which was the last thing on her mind. But she had enough insight to know that the more time they spent together, the more they *wanted* to be together. It was like an addiction. And it could only grow stronger. That was what worried her. Where would they go from here when there were so many snags in the relationship?

"Oh, I shouldn't have told you all this," she said.

He hugged her close to him. "I'm glad you did. I want a future with you, Kelly. But I'm not going to rush in like some fool and start making demands on your life. I think you've probably had enough of that."

"What are you saying?"

"I can be patient if I have to when it comes to getting what I want. My life didn't start out the way I would have chosen. There were times when none of us got enough to eat, or we didn't have money to heat the house properly. But I decided it was up to me to change it, and I did. Having you in my life now would sort of make up for all the bad times." He gazed deeply into her eyes. "I want you, Kelly, but I love you too much to see you unhappy, especially after the things you've told me about your past."

"I should never have told you all that . . . about my marriage and all. After what you went through growing up, it probably sounds petty."

He shook his head. "You're wrong about that.

What you went through was much worse." When she looked doubtful, he went on. "You see, I may have done without, but I always knew it was temporary. I had the belief in myself that I could change it. I don't know where that belief came from, but it was what pushed me on, even when it looked like I'd fail. You may have started out believing in yourself, but somewhere along the way you lost it. The good news is, I think you've found it again. But for some reason you fear you'll lose it and everything else by falling in love again, because you can't possibly hope to get as much out of the relationship as you give." He frowned in thought. "Does that make sense?"

Kelly knew he was headed in the right direction, but her insecurities went much deeper than that, as did her needs. She cocked her head to one side. "You think you've got me all figured out, don't you?"

He laughed. "Lady, I don't think a room full of psychiatrists could figure you out completely, but I'll bet I'm close." He touched her nose with the tip of his finger. "I've had my share of doubts and fears and insecurities. Everybody has them from time to time."

"I find it hard to believe you ever lacked confidence."

"Listen, I've wheeled and dealed with men who had degrees I couldn't pronounce. I never even graduated from high school, Kelly. If it weren't for my secretary, I couldn't put a business letter together without sounding like a grammatical nightmare. My lawyer walked me through contracts until I finally got the hang of it, and my accountant taught me how to manage money and protect it. And Mrs. Baxter . . ." He smiled fondly. "Mrs. Baxter taught me manners. So you see, I've had to deal with insecurities myself." He tweaked her nose as she stared at him in disbelief. "But if you tell anyone, I'll wring your neck. I don't want people to think I'm anything less than a sharp guy."

"You certainly come across well," she said. "I would never have guessed all this."

"I've had my share of coaches. They were fine people who believed in me and were happy to see me succeed. I think too much of myself to let someone treat me like a second-class citizen, and so should you."

She was quiet for a minute as she mulled over his words. "Thanks for telling me that," she finally said. "I think I needed to hear it."

When Mrs. Baxter returned, carrying a sleepy Katie, Macon loaded Kelly and her children into his car and drove them home. Once he helped tuck Katie into bed, he turned down Kelly's offer to stay for a while.

"I think we're all tired, and tomorrow's a workday," he said. "Samantha's yawning so wide I can see the fillings in her molars." He grinned at Samantha as he said it.

"Oh, yuck!" she said, wrinkling her nose. "That's the most disgusting thing I've ever heard!" She stomped down the hall to her bedroom, leaving Kelly and Macon laughing at the front door.

"Welcome to the family," Kelly said. "She thinks the rest of us are gross too."

Macon kissed her good night. "I'm going to miss you in my bed," he whispered, "but maybe if I'm lucky, the sheets will still smell like you. Don't forget to lock up." With that he was gone.

Kelly watched him drive away, a thoughtful look on her face. How many times had Bob reminded her to lock the doors at night? It used to irritate the daylights out of her because she thought it was his way of saying she was irresponsible, that he couldn't trust her with the care of his children while he was out of town. Just as he'd told her not to drive the children in the fog or rain, or when the roads were icy. She had always gritted her teeth in annoyance. But when Macon said things like that, it didn't bother her. In fact, she was warmed by his concern. How could the same simple request sound so different coming from two men?

She closed the door and locked it, then made her way through the house, switching off lights. Thoughts were beginning to open in her mind, unfolding like a handkerchief that had been pressed into a tiny square. For some reason, it was important that she examine those thoughts, like why she'd gotten angry with Macon for sending over the lawn service and for showing up later to cut her grass. She'd taken it as a personal affront, that he didn't think her capable of doing things for herself. In the past whenever she'd gotten behind and Bob had chipped in to help, she'd felt incompetent. Macon had pointed out his reasons simply enough—that he'd wanted to spend the day with her and was ready to help in order to free up her time.

Kelly gazed into the empty kitchen as if expecting a vision to appear and answer the questions popping up in her head. The million-dollar one was, had Bob purposefully tried to make her feel like cow manure or had she done it to herself? After a long moment Kelly laughed. "Probably both of us," she said aloud.

It made perfect sense, she decided after further thought. Given Bob's personality, his being a bit of a perfectionist and always wanting to be in control, and given the fact that she was often intimidated by him, she had let his slightest comment snowball in her mind until she no longer had much faith in herself.

But that was the past. Macon had told her to go easy on herself, and he was right. She had to learn to be her own best friend. She owed it to herself as well as to her children.

With this knowledge she marched down the hall to her bedroom and picked up the telephone. She dialed Margie's number frantically, her fingers trembling from her excitement. The telephone was picked up on the third ring.

Kelly didn't waste any time. "Margie, it's me," she said without preamble. "You know how you're always accusing me of having a complex? Well,

I've got it all figured out! I'm not such a bad person after all, I've just been telling myself that all these years. Bob didn't do it to me, I did it to myself. I'm responsible for my own feelings, Margie, not anyone else. Do you know how good that makes me feel?" She almost shouted the words. "It means I don't have to please anybody but myself. And I like myself, Margie, I really do. No, I *love* myself! I could actually hug myself right now. What do you think of that?" She stopped to catch her breath.

There was a grunt from the other end of the line. "Who in the hell is this!" a man demanded gruffly.

The voice startled her so much, Kelly almost dropped the telephone. "Oh, I'm sorry!" she exclaimed. "I must've dialed the wrong number."

Macon returned home to find Mrs. Baxter setting up the automatic coffeemaker, having already thoroughly cleaned the kitchen.

"Nice lady, that Mrs. Garrett," she said when he entered the room. "Very nice. And so are the children."

"Hmm." He pulled out a kitchen chair and sank onto it, feeling very tired. But the thought of climbing into his empty bed depressed him. Perhaps he'd work for a while. He always had that to fall back on. Somehow, hard work took his focus off himself. It made him feel important, as though he were contributing something to this life.

Mrs. Baxter turned to face him. "Are you in love with her?"

The question surprised him, and he didn't answer right away. "Yes, I am," he finally said.

"I thought so. You couldn't take your eyes off her all evening." She ambled to the table and sat down, folding her large hands together. "She's no bigger than a June bug," she continued, chuckling, "but the prettiest little thing I've seen in a long time." When he didn't answer, she pursed her lips in irritation. "Aren't you going to say anything?"

Macon gazed at the woman sitting across from him, a half smile playing on his lips. Mrs. Baxter had worked for him for five years and was the closest thing he had to a mother. Sure, there was his aunt who'd raised him, but she had children of her own. Mrs. Baxter had only her sister. Although the woman had long insisted he call her by her first name, he'd always referred to her as Mrs. Baxter. He did it partly to tease her, but mainly to show respect. And he had a lot of respect for her.

"What do you want me to say?" he asked.

She smiled slyly. "Is it serious? Do I hear wedding bells?" She cupped one hand to her ear as if to listen.

It was what Mrs. Baxter lived for, Macon knew, but she had never really encouraged it with most women he'd invited over. But then, most women weren't Kelly. Just saying her name in his mind conjured up thoughts of softness and sweetness.

He cleared his throat and straightened in his chair, feeling like a schoolboy under Mrs. Baxter's scrutiny. "I don't know what's going to happen. I don't think I have a whole lot to offer Kelly when it comes to—to things that really matter."

"What you're saying is your money doesn't mean squat to her."

He grinned. "I guess that's one way of putting it."

"What *is* important to her, then?"

"Things like family and togetherness. She wants a full-time husband and father, and I don't think she'll settle for less. Even if she would, I'd hate like hell to let her down."

Mrs. Baxter didn't say anything right away. At last, she asked, "Does that mean you're going to stop seeing her?"

Her words hit him hard, like a brick in the face. For a moment, he just sat there, looking and feeling very vulnerable. It was new to him, and it shook him to the core. "I don't think I can," he finally said.

Seven

Kelly and Macon had several more dates over the next couple of weeks, and he was at her house much of the time when he was in town. The children grumbled when their mother made plans that didn't include them, but Kelly didn't feel the least bit guilty. She always made special time for them when Macon was out of town, and again on weekends, when they could all be together.

One Wednesday, Kelly skipped her lunch hour so she could leave work early for a hair appointment. As she stepped inside the exclusive downtown salon, she was reminded of the vast difference between it and where she normally went for a nine-dollar trim. It didn't look like a salon at all, the waiting room carpeted and wallpapered, filled with elaborate Queen Anne furnishings and lit by a low-hanging crystal chandelier. It certainly didn't smell like one either, she noted. There were no telltale odors of perm creams or hairspray, nor the steady hum of dryers that often drowned out conversation. It resembled the lobby of a fine hotel.

"May I help you?"

Kelly turned around and found herself staring at a lovely young woman dressed in a smart business suit. "I have an appointment," she said, "with a Mr. Leonard."

"Have you ever been here before?"

"No, I haven't. A girl from work gave me his name. I managed to get in on a cancellation."

"You're very lucky. Mr. Leonard's appointments are usually scheduled six to eight weeks in advance." The woman smiled, showing movie-star teeth. "Would you like a glass of wine while you wait?"

Kelly formed a refusal on her lips but stopped. "Yes, as a matter of fact, I would." And why shouldn't she? This was her one big treat, a gift she was giving herself. It might be months before she could do anything like it again.

"Please make yourself comfortable," the woman said. "I'll be right back." She disappeared through a doorway.

Kelly took a seat on a plump rose-colored sofa with cream throw pillows. A Queen Anne coffee table of highly polished cherry held an array of glossy magazines, all of them recent issues. As she selected one, she glanced around her. There were only two other women in the room, each of them leafing through a book on hairstyles.

The young lady returned carrying Kelly's wine. "I hope you like Chablis," she said, handing her the long-stemmed glass. "It's what most of our clients prefer. Mr. Leonard is right on schedule today, so you should be able to go in shortly."

Ten minutes later Kelly was ushered into a private room bearing a chair and a wide mirror, and was greeted by a man wearing an off-white linen suit who introduced himself simply as Mr. Leonard.

"What happened to your hair, Mrs. Garrett?" he asked as soon as he'd seated her.

Kelly glanced up, startled. "I beg your pardon?"

"It's rather dull and lifeless. Have you been ill?" He fingered it gently, as though afraid it would come loose from her scalp.

She blushed. "No, I—"

"Had a baby recently?"

She gritted her teeth. "No, Mr. Leonard, I haven't been sick. I'm a mother of three children, and I don't have a lot of extra time and money to spend on my hair." She winced inwardly as she said it, waiting for the man to boot her right out of his swanky cubbyhole.

Instead he smiled. "My mother raised five boys by herself, so I know where you're coming from. But this ain't Woolworth's, honey, so it's going to cost you."

"H-how much?"

He pondered it. "How much can you afford?"

"I really can't go over fifty dollars."

"Hmm. I can shampoo and set it for fifty."

"Would it be a whole lot extra for a trim? You wouldn't have to take much off, just the ends."

"You need a body perm, you know. It's limp."

"For that I'd have to mortgage my house," she said, laughing to keep her embarrassment from showing. She was definitely in the wrong place.

"I like your sense of humor, Kelly," Mr. Leonard said, studying her reflection. "Most of the women who come in here are afraid to smile. Gives them laugh lines, don't you know?" He paused, glancing over his shoulder as if to make sure they were alone. "Tell you what. You give me seventy-five dollars and I'll make a new woman out of you. How's that?"

Kelly thought about it. That meant Katie and Joey would have to hold off a couple of weeks on their new sneakers. Not that it would warp their personalities or anything, but Kelly wasn't used to spending money on herself. Well, what about all those times she'd given herself a trim over the bathroom sink? That should count for something, shouldn't it? Didn't she deserve to splurge on herself now and then? Darn right she did. That's what being your own best friend was all about. Besides, as long as she bought the shoes before school started, what did it matter?

"You've got yourself a deal, Mr. Leonard."

He patted her shoulder, obviously pleased with her decision. "Just call me David. But don't tell anybody I said you could." He peeked around the doorway and yelled for the girl who'd given Kelly her wine. "Cancel my five o'clock appointment.

This woman's a mess! It'll take me the rest of the afternoon to clean her up." He then shrugged off his jacket and went to work.

When Kelly walked into her house three hours later, her children did a double take.

"Mom, you look fantastic!" Samantha exclaimed, circling her mother, touching a perky curl here and there. "And you look so . . . young. At least five years younger."

Kelly was equally pleased with her hair. After giving her a body perm, David had cut it in a flattering style and applied a new kind of mousse to take out the brassy color and soften it. He'd combed it back from her face with his fingers, and her natural curls fell into place in a beguiling but unfettered look. He'd then called in a young cosmetologist and insisted she show Kelly the correct way to shape her eyes with liner and shadow.

"Mr. Leonard said I looked ten years younger," Kelly said, pretending to preen. "Of course, that was after I gave him every dime to my name. Do you really think it looks okay?"

"Macon will love it. He's called twice."

Kelly's ears perked at the information. Macon had been out of town since Monday, and she'd missed him terribly. He'd called twice since leaving, but it wasn't the same.

She suddenly remembered her vow to stop trying to please other people. "I didn't get my hair done for Macon," she said matter-of-factly. "I did it for me." Then, because it was difficult to break old habits, she added, "You really think he'll like it?"

"You'll be able to find out for yourself in a little while. He said he'd meet us at Joey's game as soon as his plane landed."

"Joey's game?" Kelly shrieked. "I forgot all about it!" She glanced at her wristwatch. "I'm running the concession stand tonight and I'm supposed to be there in fifteen minutes." She threw her hands up in the air. "Joey, put on your baseball uniform. And hurry! We don't have a minute to spare."

"You didn't iron it."

She rolled her eyes heavenward. "You'll have to wear it wrinkled then." Not that anyone would notice, since he spent all of his time on the bench. "Samantha, clean Katie up and put her in the car while I get out of these clothes. We'll have to grab a hot dog at the game. And you say Macon is definitely coming?" she called over her shoulder as she raced down the hall, stepping out of her heels.

Samantha grabbed Katie by the hand, already leading her in the direction of the bathroom. "Uh-huh. I gave him directions, but he said he'd probably be late."

"So what else is new?" Kelly mumbled.

She made the drive to the ball park in record time. After handing Katie over to Samantha and wishing Joey luck, she ran to the concession stand, where she found one of the other team mothers already at work.

"Sorry I'm late, Doris," Kelly said as she washed her hands in a tiny sink at the back of the room.

"No problem. I just got here myself. Hey, your hair looks nice."

"I just had it done."

"Too bad you have to work in this place tonight. In fifteen minutes it'll look as bad as mine."

Doris had been right, Kelly noted after a while. By the time the game was half over, her hair was hanging in her eyes, limp from the heat. The back of her blouse was plastered to her skin. The oscillating fan sitting next to the ice cream machine did little to alleviate the heat inside the small room, and Kelly began to fantasize about the long shower she would take when she returned home. She handed a man his order and dropped his money into a metal cash box, then turned around to see Macon's smiling face. He looked quite handsome standing there in his wrinkled dress shirt, open at the collar and the sleeves rolled up to his elbows.

"Hi, beautiful," he said. "I tried to call you from the plane but I'm beginning to find out that keeping up with your schedule is more difficult than keeping up with mine. Did you have to work late?"

"I had my hair done."

He glanced at her damp, unruly hair and nodded as though it made complete sense. "I see."

"It sort of fell down, I guess," she said, patting the back and sides. "What can I get you?"

"What do you recommend?"

She laughed. "That you find another place to eat."

He grinned and leaned forward on the counter. "I've missed you like crazy."

She was about to answer when the man behind Macon cleared his throat loudly. "I guess you'd better order."

"Yeah, I guess," he said, giving the man a dark look. "Have the girls eaten? I thought I'd buy us all a hot dog."

"Three hot dogs coming up."

"And you'd better give me three cold drinks to go with them." He waited patiently while Kelly filled the order, glancing at the ball field every now and then. "Who's winning the game?"

Kelly located a small cardboard box and stacked his order inside so he'd be able to carry it all. "The other team."

"As usual," Doris mumbled beside her.

Macon smiled. "I don't see Joey."

"He's in the dugout with my son," Doris said.

"As usual," Kelly added. "That'll be five dollars and twenty cents."

He handed her a twenty-dollar bill. "Why isn't he playing?" he asked as she got his change.

She shrugged. "The coach doesn't think he's good enough." She counted out his money. "The girls are sitting on the top row of the bleachers. Samantha's wearing a white T-shirt with giant red lips on the front. You can't miss them."

"Giant lips, huh? Boy, does that conjure up some wicked ideas." He picked up his order and winked. "See you after the game."

"Who's the hunk?" Doris asked after Macon

had gone. "I don't believe I've seen him around here before."

Kelly didn't look up as she put another order together. "Oh, he's just a guy from work."

"What line of work is he in?"

"Construction."

"A construction worker, huh? Well, I suppose there's nothing wrong with that. My sister married one. Just be sure you don't quit your own job if things get serious. You can't always depend on him finding work."

Once things slowed down, Doris and Kelly grabbed hot dogs for themselves and chatted for a few minutes while they ate. "Why don't you go ahead and leave," Doris suggested. "It's almost time to close up anyway." Kelly didn't waste any time arguing; she was eager to be with Macon. As she thanked Doris, she prepared a hot dog for Joey so he could eat as soon as the game was over."

"I owe you one, Doris," she called as she left. "See you next week."

Kelly found Macon sitting on the top bleacher with Katie in his lap. The little girl looked as though she could drift off to sleep without any trouble. Macon seemed absorbed in the game but smiled when he saw Kelly.

"Where's Samantha?" she asked, taking a seat beside him.

"She saw some friends from school she wanted to sit with. She said she'd meet us here after the game. How come Joey isn't playing, Kelly? He

can't be any worse than the rest of these kids."
He'd barely gotten the words out of his mouth
when the couple in front of them turned around
and glared at him.

"Shhh!" Kelly leaned close. "You'd better watch
what you say or you're going to have a fight on
your hands," she whispered.

"Sorry."

Katie tugged Macon's shirt and he looked down.
"Samantha says Joey couldn't hit a ball if it was
the size of a cow," the girl told him.

Kelly pursed her lips in irritation. "Samantha
could use a dose of good manners."

"Is he really that bad?" Macon asked.

"He could use some work, but I'm scared of the
ball. Every time I throw it to him, I cower for fear
he'll actually hit it."

"I could work with him if you like," Macon
suggested.

"You?"

"You sound surprised. I know a little about
baseball."

"But when would you find time?"

He shrugged. "How about tomorrow? I could
pick up something from the store to throw on the
grill and—"

"Macon, before you start making plans, I should
tell you, I signed up for an advanced accounting
course at the community college. I start tomorrow
night from seven until nine, twice a week."

"Do you *have* to take it?"

"Yes, I do. I'd been out of the job market for so

long that I offered to take a brush-up course when I was hired. I can't very well back out now."

"Well, I'll work it out somehow. We can't have the boy sitting on the bench all season."

"We'll see." Kelly decided not to press him. She didn't want Macon making promises to her son that he couldn't keep. Joey had had enough of that to last him a lifetime.

Macon filled her in on his business trip while they watched the last few minutes of the game, and Katie drifted off to sleep. He shook his head at the sight. "Boy, this kid dozes at the drop of a hat."

"I wish I could fall asleep that easily," Kelly said.

He grinned. "You could if you didn't have such a guilty conscience."

She poked him in the ribs. "I didn't have a guilty conscience until I met you, Rambo." She giggled, then swallowed when the couple in front of them shot curious glances over their shoulders. "C'mom, let's get out of here. The game's over, and we're a dismal failure once again."

When they arrived back at Kelly's, Macon carried Katie inside. Kelly had to wrestle the sleepy girl into the bathroom to brush her teeth and wash up before climbing into bed.

"I have to take a quick shower," Kelly said to Macon. "Why don't you watch TV. I won't be but a minute. Fix yourself something cold to drink if you like."

She hurried down the hall, already anticipating

her shower. When she stepped out a few minutes later feeling like a different person, she dried herself and slipped on her bathrobe. She returned to the den and halted at the door. Macon, stretched out on the couch with his shoes kicked off, was snoring fitfully.

"Jet lag," Samantha said, coming up behind Kelly. "Daddy used to have it all the time, remember?"

Kelly leaned against the door frame and sighed. "How could I forget? It took all weekend for him to catch up on his rest, then he had to turn around and do it all over again."

"What are you going to do?"

"Think we can wake him?"

Samantha shook her head. "He looks dead to the world to me. Why don't you let him stay?"

Kelly glanced at her daughter. "You mean spend the night?"

"That old couch is as comfortable as a bed. Daddy used to sleep on it all the time."

"Very funny." Kelly gazed at the sleeping man, noting how handsome and peaceful he looked. And how utterly sexy. "I wonder if Mrs. Baxter is expecting him home? I suppose I should call her."

"Mom, are you in love with Macon?"

The question caught Kelly off guard. She stuttered and stammered a bit, then finally managed to say, "Yes, I am. Do you mind?"

The girl shook her head. "Not if it makes you this happy." She studied her mother with unveiled curiosity. "You seem different somehow. But

better. I just don't want you to be like you were
with Daddy. I want you to be careful. Isn't that
what you always tell me?"

Kelly took her daughter's hand and squeezed it.
"I promise."

When Kelly's ex-husband called the following
Saturday and offered to take the children for the
weekend, she had mixed feelings. In the end, she
decided to let them go, hoping it would bring
them all closer as a result. The children were
waiting for their father when he arrived, each
holding an overnight bag. Kelly let Bob in and
smiled at him, noting how much he'd aged over
the past few years. Dark circles beneath his eyes
made him look tired. His light brown hair had
thinned considerably and his waistline was thicker.
It was surprising, considering he'd always been
acutely aware of his looks.

"How have you been, Bob?" she asked politely
once he'd hugged the children.

He returned her smile, but it didn't quite reach
his eyes. "Fine. And you? You look different."

"I got my hair cut."

"It's nice. But then, you always looked nice, so
that's nothing new."

She invited him to sit down. Although the conversation was a bit strained, only Katie seemed to
have a real problem. Kelly had to keep reminding
herself that her youngest had been just a baby
when her father moved out, and it was only natu-

ral for her to feel shy. But the fact that Bob had made an attempt to spend time with his children convinced Kelly she was doing the right thing by letting them go.

When it was time for them to leave, she carried Katie to the car and strapped her in, then kissed each child good-bye. She faced Bob once again. "How is . . . uh . . ." She could never remember his new wife's name.

"She's fine," he said a bit curtly. Then he looked down. "Actually, we're separated."

For a moment Kelly didn't know what to say. "Gee, I'm sorry," she said at last. "Are you sure you're up to having the kids?"

He nodded. "It beats the hell out of staring at four walls."

It wasn't exactly what Kelly wanted to hear, but she decided it would have to do. "Well, call me if there's a problem."

He didn't say anything for a moment. "Could I call you if there's not a problem?"

Kelly found herself at a loss for words once again. "I'm always there if you need a friend, Bob. You know that."

She watched them drive away, then returned to the house. Inside, it was quiet. She sank onto the sofa, kicked off her sneakers, and propped her feet on the table. There was something to be said for ex-husbands, she thought, then grinned and picked up the telephone.

Macon answered on the first ring. "What are you doing?" she asked.

"Hi, honey." He sounded happy to hear from her. "I was just going over some contracts I have to sign in Atlanta on Monday."

"I thought you were going to give up the life of a workaholic," she teased.

Macon smiled and kicked his legs up on his desk. "They say old habits die hard, but maybe you could think of something better to do. Something that requires less hard work."

She laughed. "Maybe I can. How would you like to come to my pajama party?"

"Pajama party?"

She told him about Bob taking the children for the weekend. "So you see, I have the place all to myself until tomorrow evening."

"That's the best offer I've had in a long time," he said, wondering if she could hear the grin in his voice. Here was the chance he'd been waiting for—to spend an entire night with Kelly. To wake up and find her beside him, all softness and sweetness. To open his eyes in the morning and reach for her. She would be as cuddly as a new puppy. "There's only one problem, pipsqueak. I don't like pajamas."

"Oh, that won't be a problem, Rambo, I assure you."

When Macon arrived at Kelly's place early that evening, he found her wearing a sexy negligee and the house smelling of Italian food. He let out a low wolf whistle at the sight of her and took her in his arms. She smelled faintly of soap and perfume. Her hair shone, and he caught the scent of baby shampoo. "Isn't it a bit early to be in your pajamas?" he asked, a wicked twinkle in his eyes. "It isn't even dark outside."

She snaked her arms around his neck and snuggled against him suggestively. He was aroused immediately. "I didn't invite you over to play outside," she said. "We're going to play *inside* tonight, if that's okay with you."

He answered her with a long, heated kiss.

Their lovemaking was slow and thorough. Kelly had taken the telephone off the hook so they wouldn't be disturbed with calls from Samantha's friends, and it was sheer heaven to lie in Macon's arms and not have to worry about anything but the two of them. Macon kissed her deeply, then drew lazy circles all over her with his tongue, delighting in the fact that they didn't have to hurry. When he entered her, they both gasped aloud at the sheer pleasure of the act, and he wondered if there would ever come a time when he would sink into her softness without feeling as though he'd lose his mind. They climaxed together, Kelly crying out his name softly and he capturing the sound with his lips.

Afterward, they lay exhausted but completely satisfied. The room was quiet, painted in mauve shadows from the setting sun. The only sound was the steady ticking of the clock on the night table.

Kelly could feel herself smiling broadly. "Do I

look goofy with this big grin on my face?" she asked.

Macon squeezed her. "You look beautiful, and yes, a bit goofy." She punched him playfully. "I feel like a million bucks," he confessed. "Let's run away and get married and live happily ever after."

Kelly felt as though her stomach had just fallen to her feet. "Where would we live?" she asked, wondering if she was crazy to pursue the subject with him.

He pondered it for a while. "I could probably convince the architect in Houston to design us a house," he finally said. "A big Victorian house with wide porches and tall windows to let in plenty of sunlight. We'd fill the porches with old-fashioned rocking chairs and hang big pots of ferns out there and—" He grinned. "We'd put a telephone in every room for Samantha."

"And we'd build the house in one of those chic neighborhoods where everybody drives a BMW," she added glumly, "and then my family would feel out of place when they came to visit."

He laughed. "No, we wouldn't. We'd build it out in the country so we could have farm animals and a million pets if we wanted. Just like you had growing up. We'd buy a hound dog and assign him the job of sleeping on the front porch so we had to step over him every time we carried in the groceries."

"What about Mrs. Baxter?"

"Would you mind very much if we took her with

us? She loves you and the kids and we'd need the help."

"Of course not. I'd probably welcome the company. After all, you'd be gone all the time." Kelly felt like a heel bringing it up, but she couldn't help herself. What Macon described sounded like a dream, but it was too good to be true. He had the funds to build her such a home, but he wouldn't be there to share it with her, so what did it matter? He was still her boss, top dog of one of the biggest construction companies in the country. His responsibilities were staggering. But she didn't like to think of that because it left her feeling even more unsure of their relationship, as though her time with him was only temporary. How could she hope to have a future with such a man?

Macon's excitement ebbed at her words. "Kelly, you don't give an inch."

"Inches turn into miles before you know it." she said simply. "And then you find you're giving a lot more than you get back."

"I thought you knew me better than that."

She rose up on one elbow and gazed down at him, thinking as she always did how utterly handsome he was. "Macon, I want to use this time just to be together. We can talk about the future tomorrow. Tomorrow the kids will be back and things will turn crazy again. Couldn't we just savor this moment and not have to worry about who we are or what we are or how we're going to spend the rest of our lives?"

Macon knew he had to back off, but dammit, he wanted to make plans with her, he wanted to talk about the future. Still, he'd promised not to rush her, and he knew the obstacles in her mind were very real. Instead of persisting, he merely smiled. "I love you, Kelly Garrett," he said, taking her into his arms once again, "and I can't wait to wake up tomorrow and find you lying beside me. But right now I'm starved, and I smell something very tempting coming from your kitchen."

She bolted upright in the bed. "The lasagna! It's probably dry as the Sahara Desert by now." Although Kelly had had the foresight to turn the oven temperature down low, she hadn't counted on spending two hours in bed with Macon. She grabbed Macon's shirt and threw it on. Buttoning it haphazardly, she raced down the hall toward the kitchen.

Luckily, the lasagna was okay. She pulled the tossed salad she'd made earlier from the refrigerator, topped it with artichoke hearts, fresh scallions, and mushrooms, and set it on the table while Macon opened the wine. He'd stepped into his jeans, but since Kelly was wearing his shirt, he was naked from the waist up. She informed him that was the way she preferred it. His shirt was big on her and hung open slightly, offering him a delightful peek at the white valley between her breasts.

They were both ravenous and did justice to the meal as well as to the bottle of wine. They returned to bed without cleaning the kitchen, and after making love once more, fell asleep in each other's arms.

Kelly snuggled deeper under the covers, trying to ignore the sounds barging into her sleep. She thought she heard Macon's voice and smiled dreamily.

"Kelly, honey, wake up. Somebody's at the front door."

"What?" She opened her eyes and found it was still dark. Blinking at Macon, she felt as though a fog had settled around her brain. Too much wine the night before. Her head ached. "What is it?" she asked dumbly.

"Somebody is ringing your doorbell." As if acting on cue, the doorbell sounded again. "Do you want me to answer it?" He was already up, grabbing his jeans from the floor.

Kelly sat up and reached for the closest thing to cover herself with, which just happened to be Macon's shirt again. "What time is it?" she asked, searching frantically for her panties. She found them under one of Macon's sneakers.

"Six o'clock."

"Oh, jeez. Who in their right mind . . . ?" She didn't finish the sentence as she stumbled down the hall and to the front door with Macon on her heels. She groped for the switch and turned on the porch light, then peered through the peephole. "Oh, no."

"Who is it?" Macon asked.

"It's Bob. He's got the kids with him." The bell rang again and she turned to Macon. "What should I do?"

He muttered a curse under his breath. "You'll have to let them in, honey."

"Macon, my children are out there with him. What'll they think?"

He raked his hands through his hair. "Open the door, Kelly. One of them could be sick. We'll have to deal with the rest later."

Kelly hadn't considered that possibility, but the thought that one of her children might be hurting was more important than her own embarrassment. Without wasting another second she unlocked the door and threw it open. Bob was holding a sleeping Katie in his arms. Samantha and Joey stood beside him.

Kelly didn't waste a moment on the preliminaries. "What's wrong?" she asked, quickly scanning all three children.

Bob scowled. He looked tired and angry. "Katie hasn't slept all night. I tried to call, but the line was busy."

Kelly remembered suddenly that she'd forgotten to put the telephone back on the hook. "Is she sick?"

"No, just homesick. Have you been on the phone all night, for Pete's sake?" Bob stepped inside, then did a double take when he saw Macon.

Kelly followed his gaze and blushed a bright red

at the sight of Macon, bare-chested, his jeans riding low on his hips, his hair tousled from sleep. Samantha and Joey came in behind their father and came to an abrupt standstill when they, too, saw Macon.

"What's going on, Kelly?" Bob demanded.

She didn't miss his accusatory tone or the self-righteous look on his face. From where they stood, they could see into the kitchen, which was still a mess from the night before. It looked, for all the world, like a great orgy had taken place. Kelly wanted to crawl under a rock.

Eight

"This is Macon Bridges," Kelly said at last, trying to muster every bit of dignity she had left. "Macon, this is Bob Garrett, my ex-husband."

The men nodded curtly at each other. For another long minute everyone merely stared at one another.

Samantha was the first to speak. "I don't know about the rest of you, but I'm going to bed," she announced. "Mom, Katie cried all night," she added before disappearing down the hall. Joey mumbled something and followed.

Kelly's heart turned as she took a closer look at her youngest, whose eyes were swollen from crying. She was overcome with such a feeling of guilt that she thought she would be sick, then she realized it must be from all the wine she'd drunk the night before. More guilt followed. "Bob, would you please carry Katie to her bedroom."

He nodded and made his way down the hall, with Kelly following close behind, to the bedroom Katie and Samantha shared. The older girl was lying on her bed, fully dressed, already asleep.

Neither of them spoke while Kelly tucked the little girl in bed. Katie opened her eyes once and smiled when she saw her mother, then stuck her thumb between her lips and fell back asleep. When she straightened, Kelly found Bob watching her.

"This is a fine surprise, Kelly," he said, his voice a furious whisper. "I don't know what to say."

She faced him squarely. "Don't say anything, then."

"Don't you care what the children think, for heaven's sake? What about Samantha? Just look at you."

"I know what I look like," Kelly said, trying to keep her own voice low despite her rising anger. "And yes, I care very much what my children think. You should have thought about that before you walked out and moved in with what's-her-name."

"Her name is Julianne, and she has nothing to do with this."

"I don't care what her name is, but you're right, she has absolutely nothing to do with this. This is between you and me. I'm sick to death of your standing in judgment of everything I do. What I do is none of your business."

"It's my business when it concerns my children," he said, giving her a smug look. "If you don't think you can be a proper mother—"

"Would you like to take them, Bob?" she asked sweetly, resisting the urge to slap his face. "Perhaps you'd like to have custody. Why don't we call our lawyers and see what we can arrange?" She knew it wasn't likely he'd go along with the idea. Bob liked his freedom too much.

"I'd never take the children from you, Kelly. I know what it would do to you."

"You're all heart." Sarcasm dripped from her voice.

"You've changed, Kelly."

She smiled. "I certainly hope so." When she looked up, she saw Macon standing in the doorway. She wondered how much of the conversation he'd heard.

"Joey decided he was hungry, so I fixed him some toast," he said, smiling at her. "And the coffee is ready." He glanced at Bob. "Sorry you can't join us."

Bob was clearly taken aback at the subtle invitation to leave. "I hope you know what you're doing," he said to Kelly. Then, with a long last look at her, he was gone.

Kelly and Macon sipped their coffee at the kitchen table while Joey filled them in on what had happened the night before. "And then Katie got so upset she threw up in the bed," he said between bites of toast. "I thought Dad was going to go right through the ceiling. He made Samantha get off the phone and help him clean up. Then

Katie refused to go back to sleep. When Dad couldn't get you on the phone, he called Julianne to come over and help, and she couldn't make Katie stop crying either. But I think she and Dad made up before he brought us home."

Kelly reached over and brushed a sandy curl from her son's face. "Are you tired?"

"A little."

"Why don't you go to sleep?"

"Macon said he'd play ball with me."

"How about we do it tomorrow?" Macon suggested, giving Kelly a slight smile. "I think we're all tired today. I have to be in Atlanta for a meeting in the morning, but I should be back in time to practice before it gets dark."

"Fine with me," the boy said eagerly. He popped the rest of the toast into his mouth and looked at his mother. "Is it okay if I just lie on the couch for a while?" She nodded.

When Kelly and Macon were finally alone, he took her hand and kissed it. "I'm sorry about all this," he said. "I would have done anything to prevent it."

"I know."

"We can talk to Samantha together if you like. I think once we explain how we feel about each other, she'll understand."

"I'll talk to her after she wakes up."

He nodded. "Whatever you think is best." He stood and stretched, then drained his coffee cup. "Why don't I go home and let you go back to bed? I'll call you after I take a shower and we can plan to do something later."

"Macon, I think I'd just like to hang around the house today if you don't mind. I have to take Katie and Joey out to find new shoes later, and I have no idea how long it'll take."

He knelt before her and took both hands in his. "Do me a favor, honey," he said, his eyes searching hers. "Don't let that bastard walk in here and tell you how to run your life. You were doing a fine job without any help from him."

"I can take care of Bob," she said, totally confident that she could.

Kelly went back to bed after Macon left, but sleep was impossible. She got up, showered and dressed, and went into the kitchen to clean up the dinner dishes. At least Macon had stacked them in the sink during her confrontation with Bob. As she puttered about the house, she couldn't seem to shake the desolate mood that had settled over her with Bob's arrival that morning, and it merely worsened as the day wore on. Fortunately, her talk with Samantha went well. The girl didn't seem to feel she was owed an explanation.

"I know you love Macon, Mom," she said, "and that he loves you. You taught me a long time ago that sex was okay when you loved someone." The bright blush on her mother's face didn't deter her in the least. "I hope I can find a man I love that much one day, but I wouldn't let anything Daddy said bother you."

"Did you hear us argue?"

"I wasn't really asleep. I heard everything he said to you. I wanted to come to your rescue, but you seemed to be doing a good job on your own. I'm glad you stood up to him. It sort of makes up for all those times you didn't."

Macon called later that day to see how she was, but Kelly, who'd spent several hours with her children at the mall shopping for shoes, was too tired to make plans. "I think I'll just fix sandwiches for dinner and call it an early night," she said, still unable to shake her glum mood and nagging headache.

"Then I'll see you tomorrow night," he said. "Try to get some rest, honey."

The following afternoon Kelly returned home from work and found Joey watching out the front window for Macon.

"I haven't heard from him," she told her son, "but he said yesterday he'd be back at the end of the day." He'd also offered to pick up steaks for dinner, so once Kelly had showered and changed, she put potatoes in the oven to bake and tossed a salad.

Kelly's mood had not improved. If anything, it had deteriorated. Although Bob's visit the day before was partially responsible for it, she knew she was past caring what he thought of her. She had come a long way from the woman whose very life had depended on pleasing him. Bob Garrett, with all his problems and deficiencies, was the last person who should offer her advice.

Kelly's glumness stemmed mostly from how *she*

felt about her life. It was going nowhere. She was in love with a man who was not capable of providing the kind of life she'd always yearned for. Although she knew Macon loved her, he would always be just beyond her grasp. There would always be meetings and business trips and unexpected phone calls. It would be like having a relationship with a married man, she supposed. They would have to steal what time they could find. She would have to be content with what he could give her for the moment and learn not to expect more than that.

And she would never be happy with such an arrangement.

By seven o'clock there was still no word from Macon, and when the telephone rang at seven-thirty, Kelly wasn't surprised to learn it was he.

"Where are you?" she asked.

"Still in Atlanta. The meeting just let out. I tried to call earlier, but the line was busy." He sounded tired. "Look, about dinner—"

"Well, it's obvious you can't make it," she interrupted.

"I'm sorry, honey. Could we do it another time?"

"It's not the dinner that matters so much, Macon," she said, feeling tired herself. "You promised to play ball with Joey."

"I never promised," he said. "I told him I'd try. I explained about the meeting."

"He was counting on you."

"Should I have just walked out of the meeting, for heaven's sake?" he asked, his voice rising out of irritation.

"Of course not. But you shouldn't have made plans with my son unless you were certain you could carry through. He's had enough of that sort of thing with his father."

"I'm tired of being blamed for what your ex-husband did, Kelly. Now, why don't you let me talk to the boy."

"So you can make more promises? No thanks. I'll take care of it myself."

"I'll come by when my plane lands."

"No, Macon. I won't be here."

"Are you going out?" He sounded surprised.

"Yes, I am. Does it surprise you that I have a life of my own?"

"Kelly, honey, let's not fight."

"I'm not fighting with you. But I'm not going to put my own life on hold until it's convenient for you to spend time with us. I did that for a long time, Macon, and I promised myself I'd never do it again. I don't deserve that kind of life, and neither do my children."

"Haven't I tried to do what you asked?" he insisted. "I mess up one time and you're ready to throw in the towel."

"You didn't mess up, Macon, I did. I've known all along it wouldn't work between us. There's nothing wrong with you. You're a very nice person, a very *successful* person. But there is no room for anything else in your life, especially a family. I have to go now."

"Kelly, wait! Don't hang up."

"I really don't have anything else to say."

"When can I see you?"

"You can't." With that, she hung up. When she turned around, she found Joey standing there, holding his baseball glove.

"That was Macon, wasn't it?"

"Yes." She knelt before her son. "Joey, Macon isn't going to be able to come after all. He—" She paused. How many times had she had to make explanations to her children, soothe the disappointment? "The meeting ran longer than he thought it would. I'm sorry. Would you mind very much if I played ball with you instead?"

Joey shook his head, looking at her as though she'd just lost all her marbles. "Mom, you're scared of the ball."

"I am not!" she said, pretending to be indignant.

"Then how come you dive to the ground every time I hit it?" He laughed finally. "If you want to play ball, that's fine with me."

She smiled brightly. "I'd consider it an honor." She turned off the oven, set the salad in the refrigerator, and followed her son outside.

Joey had been right about one thing, Kelly reminded herself as she stood before him ready to pitch to him. She was terrified of being hit. She'd been hit once as a child when playing ball with her brothers, even had a scar on her head from the stitches to prove it, and ever since then had shied away from the game completely. Luckily, Joey did not hit the ball often, but when he did, Kelly covered her head with her hands and ducked. Twice, she fell on her face, and both times cursed

Macon Bridges for all he was worth. He would not get the opportunity to disappoint her son again, she promised herself.

When it was too dark to see anymore, Kelly called the game to a halt, and they went inside to eat a late dinner. She pulled a package of hot dogs from the freezer and tossed them into the microwave so they would have something to go with the rest of the meal. Then she piled her children into the car in time to make a nine o'clock movie, knowing all the while that Katie would never last and that she herself would have a heck of a time getting up for work the next morning. But she was determined not to be home in case Macon came by.

The telephone was ringing when they stepped inside the door sometime after eleven. Kelly, who was carrying Katie in her arms, stopped Samantha from grabbing it. "Don't answer it," she said.

The look Samantha shot her mother was one of incredible disbelief. "Don't answer it?"

"I don't have time to explain," Kelly said, carrying Katie into the bedroom. "Just let it ring." Once Kelly had Katie tucked in, she went into her bedroom, took the phone off the hook, and tucked it into the top drawer of her nightstand.

Nine

When Kelly arrived home from work the following evening, Macon's car was sitting in front of her house. He didn't wait for her to get out. Instead, he strode over to her car and leaned inside her window.

"We need to talk."

Kelly tried to remain calm, but her heart was pounding like mad. "What do you want?"

"I want you to take a ride with me," he said, opening her door. "It won't take long."

"I'm sorry, but I can't."

"Please, Kelly. I have to leave tonight for Houston. We got the job on the convention center and—"

"Congratulations," she said flatly, knowing it was just another obligation that would pull him further away from her. But hadn't she known it all along? There would always be another job to bid on, another site to inspect. Macon thrived on work, it was what mattered most in his life. Those facts had been glaringly apparent from the very beginning, but she had fallen in love with him despite all that, and it was love that had kept her believing things could somehow change.

"Kelly, just do this one thing for me. I didn't sleep all night last night, and I must've picked up the phone to call you at least ten times today."

She looked up in alarm at the tone of his voice. He sounded desperate. This was not the Macon Bridges she knew, the man who exuded confidence and energy. His expression was tired and hopeless. But there she was, letting love get in the way of common sense again. What could Macon possibly have to show her that would make any difference in their circumstances? He wasn't the only one who'd missed a night's sleep. She'd spent the night convincing herself that there was no place for her in his life, and the other half sobbing quietly in her pillow, trying to exorcise him from her soul. She'd gone to work looking like hell, her concentration shot. She'd known from the beginning that her relationship would ultimately affect her work, and she'd been right.

"Kelly?"

She met his soulful gaze. What had ever made her think it would be easy putting Macon out of her life? Sending him away was like cutting a vital organ from her body. But she had to get through this somehow. She had three children who counted on her for their very existence. She could not fall apart simply because her love life was not working out. But neither could she turn her back on this man when it looked as though his insides were falling out. "I will come with you now, Macon," she said softly, "but you'll have to leave me alone afterward." He nodded and helped her from the car. "I'll have to tell Samantha," she said.

When Kelly came out a few minutes later, she found Macon standing beside his car, waiting. He opened the passenger door for her. "Where are we going?" she asked as he slid behind the wheel.

"You'll see."

He drove in silence, taking the interstate that led downtown. Kelly stared straight ahead as the car ate up the highway. Before long they had entered a rundown section of town. Tall brick buildings with wrought-iron fire escapes flanked the streets, most of them closed down and boarded up, some condemned by the city. Four-letter words had been scrawled on the buildings with garish fluorescent paint. Here and there they passed a pawnshop or adult bookstore, where neon lights flashed in chipped and broken letters.

Macon turned onto a street with shotgun-style houses squatting like tired old women behind sagging front porches. He parked in front of such a house.

"Now would you tell me what this is all about?" she asked as she stepped out of the car and glanced around anxiously. She did not feel safe there, and Macon, as though sensing as much, moved closer to her. A group of teenagers stood on the street corner smoking cigarettes, their voices rising over the sound of traffic as they called out obscenities to the passing motorists. Next door, an elderly man gazed forlornly at Kelly from his porch.

Macon motioned for her to follow him, and she did, more out of curiosity than anything else. He led her onto the front porch of the leaning clapboard house, whose exterior had little remaining paint.

"I was raised in this house by an aunt," he said, unlocking the front door and pushing it open. "My mother was only fifteen when I was born. She died of an infection when I was a week old." He stepped aside so Kelly could pass through first. "My aunt took me in, but she could barely care for her own children. I never knew my father. I guess that's not important now, but it was when I was growing up."

He paused, wondering if it had been wise just to blurt it all out like that. The only person who knew anything about his past was Mrs. Baxter, but not even she knew everything. Kelly's expression was unreadable, and he would have given everything he owned to know her thoughts.

"I've never brought anyone here before." He shrugged. "I guess I was too embarrassed."

Kelly gazed around the dim room dominated by an old wood-burning stove, thinking it really wasn't much of a room at all. It was a bleak sight, with its grimy windows that let in little of the late afternoon light. The walls were faded and gouged with holes. In silence she followed Macon across the bare wood floors, from room to room, and she shuddered at the nightmarish kitchen at the back of the house. The smell of rot and decay was everywhere.

She felt his gaze on her and looked up, willing herself to face him. "Why did you bring me here?"

"I've never had anybody that meant as much to me as you do, Kelly," he said. "I've always felt closed off from the rest of the world." He shoved his hands in his pockets and rocked back and forth on his heels for a moment. "All that changed when I met you, though. You made me feel as if I belonged."

He was silent for a moment. "Anyway, I thought by bringing you here it might help you understand why I do the things I do. I suppose living in a place like this either makes a man or breaks him. As for myself, I became very ambitious because of it." He watched her face as he spoke, wondering once again what she could be thinking. Would she think less of him now that he'd exposed his past? As much as he wished it, he could not change it, nor could he banish the memories that sometimes festered like an open wound. Kelly's love was a salve to his injuries, and he knew with time she could help him bury his past.

"I don't like money because I want a lot of things, Kelly," he went on. "I like it because of what I don't want. I don't ever want this." He made a sweeping gesture with his hands. "And I've busted my butt for twenty years to make sure of it."

She nodded slowly. "I can certainly understand,"

she said gently. "I wouldn't want this for myself, Macon, and especially not for my children." She paused before going on. Her emotions were getting the best of her, but that was what always happened when she was with Macon. She did not act on common sense, she acted on feelings. Her emotions were full now, running over the edges. Why had Macon brought her here? For sympathy? No, that wasn't his style. He'd done it for just the reason he'd said, understanding. But she would have preferred not seeing this part of his life. It hurt to think that he had ever suffered.

"You know," she said, "I once read an article someone did on Mother Teresa, who said that poverty and hunger were not the worst things that could happen to a person. She felt loneliness and isolation were much worse."

Macon eyed her cautiously. "What are you getting at?"

"I've never known poverty, but I didn't have a whole lot growing up either. We wore hand-me-downs and grew much of our own food in a garden behind our house. I never had the money to go to town with my friends and see a movie or have dinner out. My Friday nights were spent on the front porch sipping iced tea and watching the lightning bugs. I learned to make my own clothes at an early age, and if there was something special I wanted, I knew I'd have to earn the money myself. At times I resented it. I knew people in town who could afford good schools and clothes, and I was so impressed that I married a boy from one of those families."

Kelly didn't say anything for a minute, and when she did, her voice trembled with emotion. "It wasn't until then that I learned to appreciate the simple things I'd been given by my own family. I'd moved away from home to be where my husband's company needed him most. I was so lonely I thought I would die. True, I got to eat in nice restaurants now and then, but it wasn't worth the sacrifice. I really didn't have a husband, and my children didn't have a father." She smiled tightly. "But you know what it's like to be lonely. I think you've worked so hard to rise above all this that you shunned any meaningful relationship you could have had."

"I had nothing to offer back then."

"I think you did. You just didn't know it." She studied him for a moment. "Are you so much happier now that you've become a success?"

"Hell yes, I'm happier. Wouldn't you be?"

"Then that's really all that matters, isn't it?" She turned for the door.

"Wait a minute!" He grabbed her hand. "I'm not as happy as I could be, if that's what you mean," he said quickly. "And yes, I've sacrificed things like home and family, things that began to matter to me only once I'd met you. What I'm trying to say . . ." He raked his fingers through his hair. "I'd be a lot happier, thrilled, in fact, if you'd share my life with me." He pulled her into his arms. "Marry me, Kelly. That's what would make me happiest. It would make my life complete."

She stared at him, trying hard to breathe normally and control her swirling emotions. "But would it make my life complete? And what about the lives of my children?" When he didn't answer right away, she went on. "Frankly, I think I'd be right back where I started."

"I'm not your ex-husband, Kelly, and I wouldn't try to make you feel second-rate. I love you too much for that."

She knew he spoke the truth, that he would never do it intentionally. But it would happen anyway if she was forced to claw and fight for his attention, or stand in the wings and humbly accept what portion of himself he could offer. She didn't want his love rationed to her in small doses. She wanted it all. Accepting less than what she thought she deserved would be compromising her happiness once again, and she'd end up turning those feelings inward, hating herself. She had only just learned how to love herself again. She had come too far to turn back.

Kelly sighed heavily, feeling overly burdened with the decision she must make. She loved Macon with all her heart, and losing him would be like losing part of herself. Sometimes, when he held her after they made love, she didn't know where she left off and he began, that was how tied she felt to him. She'd never had that special closeness with Bob, so losing him had not devastated her as she knew losing Macon would. But being your own best friend sometimes meant making painful decisions if they were in your own best interest.

"Do you love me enough to let me go, Macon?" she asked. "Because right now I'm so vulnerable I would do anything you asked me to do. I'd marry you in a minute, because that's how much I love you."

"Kelly—"

"But next week I'd despise myself for settling for less. And I'd grow to hate you because you talked me into doing something I swore I'd never do again." She felt the rush of tears and didn't try to hide them. "If I can't be first and foremost in a man's life, then I don't want to be in his life at all."

She saw his pain in his expression, a look that mirrored her own feelings. "I don't want to be a long-distance wife, Macon. I don't want to have to sum up my life and feelings and thoughts in a three-minute phone call at the end of the day. I don't want to climb into an empty bed every night or reach out for someone and find myself alone. I would be happy married to a garbage collector as long as he came home to me at the end of the day. You say you know what you *don't* want in life, and so do I."

Macon held her for a long time, until the sobs that racked her small body quieted. He handed her his handkerchief, and she blew her nose and wiped her eyes. His own eyes ached and burned and made his head hurt. His heart felt leaden. Instead of saying anything, he pressed his lips against her forehead.

Kelly handed him his handkerchief and offered

the closest thing she had to a smile. "You have a plane to catch," she said.

Macon felt like kicking something. He had gotten nowhere with Kelly, he was losing her. Panic washed over him, making his heart thump wildly, gripping his stomach muscles like steel claws. He hated it when his stomach felt like that. It reminded him of the nights he'd tried to fall asleep as a child while his stomach growled in protest at not having enough food. But his aunt gave whatever scraps existed to her youngest, who was sickly, and Macon had thought that was right.

But Kelly Garrett fed and nourished his very soul, he suddenly realized, and he knew at that instant that a man had to feed his emotional needs as well as the physical. Yet Kelly was slipping from his grasp, and there wasn't a damn thing he could do about it. Nor could he wrap her up in a tidy bundle of aluminum foil, as he so often did with the food he felt the need to hang on to.

Macon wanted to shake her, reason with her, make her see things his way. But his plane was waiting. His pilot would have filed a flight plan, and his assistant was probably already on board. And there were people in Houston planning to meet him at the airport—lawyers, bankers, investors. Everything was in motion, each person lined up like dominoes. He didn't want to be the one to send them toppling over.

"Come on," he said in a voice that sounded nothing like his own. "I'll take you home."

Ten

The following week Macon learned there were indeed worse things in life than being poor. A broken heart was no small thing, he realized. A broken heart. Surely that was what this terrible thing was, that stole his appetite and made sleep impossible. He found himself gazing off into space during business meetings and forgetting appointments that until lately had been essential to him. He no longer cared about making a good impression, he cared only about getting through the day.

The weekend came and he saw no reason to return home. Mrs. Baxter would shake her head and cluck her tongue at him for not eating and demand to know what was going on. He wasn't ready to face her. So he worked, but even that did not take his mind off his troubles. He'd picked up the telephone a dozen times to call Kelly, then hung up. What would he say? That he loved her? Hell, she already knew that. Contrary to love songs, love did not solve all the world's problems.

He pulled out his camera and spent one afternoon taking pictures, thinking it would make him forget Kelly. It didn't, but he'd had enough of contracts and bid proposals and job specs. In the past he'd always been able to chase away his personal demons with work, but now he realized he was going to have to come to terms with his life. That made him laugh sharply. What life?

When he found in his camera bag the film he'd forgotten to develop from his weekend on the beach with Kelly, he drove immediately to a photo lab that advertised one-hour service. He waited outside as a gentle summer rain bathed the asphalt parking lot in front of the building. From time to time he peered into the window, willing the little man behind the counter to hurry. It dawned on him suddenly that he had spent a lifetime standing on the outside looking in. He was reminded of a neighborhood he used to pass through on his way home from school as a child, huddled in a jacket that was too thin to be warm. One small house always caught his eye, pristine white with blue shutters and window boxes filled with plastic geraniums. Sometimes when he passed by in the evening, light spilled from the front window, and he could see the family flocked around the kitchen table for dinner. It was this image that had haunted him in his bed at night and convinced him that

God had abandoned him, even though his aunt swore it wasn't so.

And then God had sent him an angel to love.

Macon did not look at the photographs until he'd returned to the privacy of his hotel room, and then, with a gigantic lump in his throat, he sifted through scenes of Kelly and her children that had made up the happiest two days of his life. And then, for the first time in his life, Macon Bridges cried. Silent tears ran down his face, and he could not stop them for a long time.

His day of reckoning had come. He cried for himself, for twenty years of backbreaking work with nothing to show for it. Nothing that really mattered. He cried for Kelly, understanding for the first time what it was like to truly ache for the person you loved, to reach out for her in the middle of the night and not find her. To wake up in the morning still alone. It didn't matter what a person had if there was nobody to share it with.

The following week, Macon's frustration and anger grew. He sometimes felt as though he were being pulled in a hundred different directions. It made him want to ram his fist through a wall. There were always people around him—executives, engineers, secretaries. Hell, why was he running around like a chicken with no head? Couldn't any of these people make a decision without him? One afternoon he voiced that question to his assistant. Duncan Block had been with him for years. Duncan and Hannah, his secretary, worked more closely with him than anyone else.

Duncan was obviously surprised at Macon's outburst. "If you don't mind my saying so . . ." He paused and adjusted his horn-rimmed glasses. "You've never really given anyone the opportunity to make a decision on their own. You've always wanted to be in the middle of things. You have that right, of course. It's your company."

Macon pondered Duncan's words. There was some truth to them, he finally realized. He'd always made the decisions, despite having enough sharp men on the payroll to do some of it for him. He got involved in all the bid hearings despite having qualified men to do it for him. He personally flew to job sites, even though he employed some of the best project managers money could buy.

He chuckled to himself after a moment. "I guess I haven't grown with the company," he said. "In the beginning it was only natural that I be involved in everything. When the company was small, and I didn't have many employees. But there's no excuse for that now."

Duncan shrugged. "I guess it depends on what you want."

"Or don't want," Macon said. He didn't want to live without Kelly. He couldn't. He'd spent a lifetime bemoaning his past and running away from it, but he realized now that it was his future he should concentrate on. He stood and paced the room for a bit. "Get my plane ready. Then call the office and schedule a meeting first thing the next morning. I want all my top people there. And call my housekeeper and tell her I'll be home for dinner." He smiled for the first time in days. "I'm ready to go home."

"Yes, sir." Duncan smiled broadly. "It's good to have you back, Macon."

Kelly grabbed another shirt from the ironing basket and sprayed the collar with starch before pressing the hot iron to it. She glanced up at the television set where David Letterman was interviewing a guest.

"Do you know what time it is?" Margie asked. She yawned, then settled herself more comfortably on the couch. "Surely you're not going to iron all night. Besides, you have to get up for work tomorrow."

"So do you, Margie. Which is why I remind you every night that you don't have to sit up with me. I'm fine, really."

Margie sat up and stretched. "Well, you look like hell, if you don't mind my saying so. In fact, you look worse than you did after your divorce. Why don't you just sit down and have a good cry over it? You'd feel better."

"I have cried, believe me. That's all I've done for two weeks."

"How are the kids taking it?"

"Samantha and Joey aren't saying much, but I can tell they miss Macon. Katie's the only one who asks about him. I was a fool to get my kids involved." She sighed heavily. "So foolish."

"You're not foolish," Margie insisted. "You're simply in love for the first time in your life."

Kelly swallowed past the lump in her throat. "I should have made a few compromises. But I had to be stubborn and insist on my way because I felt I'd been cheated in the past. I kept comparing him to Bob."

"That's only natural. Every time I meet a man I compare him to my ex."

"Macon is nothing like Bob, though. He's kind and considerate. He's . . ." She paused. A fat tear fell onto her cheek and slid down it. "He's the best thing that ever happened to me."

"Well, look at the bright side," Margie said. "You believed in something and you stuck to it." She shrugged. "Of course, there's no prize being offered for it, so what did you gain?"

Margie was right on the money as usual, Kelly thought. By walking away from Macon, she could feel content in the knowledge that she was holding firm to her beliefs. She had refused to give an inch, simply because she'd felt robbed in the past. She had won the battle with Macon, but now what did it matter? She had ended up with nothing.

Macon leaned back in his chair, thankful that the intense four-hour meeting had finally ended. His secretary and assistant, sitting directly across from him, looked equally relieved to have it behind them. "How do you think it went?" he finally asked.

Duncan was the first to speak. "I think your staff will be only too happy to take on their new responsibilities. They're good people. There's no question in my mind they can handle it."

"I agree, Mr. Bridges," Hannah said. "And I think you're wise to hire extra personnel. I've often said you do the work of three men."

"Yes, well, I never had a reason not to. Which reminds me, did you call the jeweler?"

She nodded. "Yes, sir. He said he'd drop by your house tonight with some fine rings for you to look at. And I was finally able to get through to the architect in Houston. He said he would do some preliminary sketches of the type of house you described and fly up with them in a few days so you and your . . . intended could mull over them."

"So when's the wedding?" Duncan asked enthusiastically.

Macon shifted uncomfortably in his chair. "I haven't exactly asked her yet. Well, I have asked her, but she sort of ignored me."

"Ignored you, sir?" Hannah said it as though she found that difficult to believe.

"That was before I had anything to offer her," Macon said.

Hannah nodded. "I see." It was clear she did not. She stood and smoothed her skirt. "If you don't need anything further, Mr. Bridges, I think I'll go to lunch."

• • •

Kelly stepped off the elevator and paused at the sight of Frederick, the security guard. Then she squared her shoulders. "I'm here to see Macon Bridges," she announced.

"Do you have an appointment?" he asked, glancing at the clipboard in his hand.

"He'll see me." She marched past him, across the reception area and Hannah's office, and halted at the door that led to Macon's office. She knocked, and the door was opened a minute later by Macon himself.

He was too stunned to say anything at first. "Kelly, honey, what a surprise."

"Macon, we have to talk," she said matter-of-factly. "I'm on my lunch hour, so I don't have much time."

"Sure, Kelly. Come in and sit down." It was all he could do to keep from hauling her into his arms after almost two weeks of not seeing her. Damn, he'd missed her. The navy suit she wore flattered the delicate lines of her body, though he suspected she'd lost weight. She looked tired, and dark circles marred her eyes. She seemed smaller somehow, sad and vulnerable, like a broken bird. He wanted to sweep her into his arms and carry her away to a safe place. Instead, he closed the door and led her to the sofa. Once they were seated, Kelly didn't waste any time.

"I was wrong, Macon. It took me a while to see that. I ironed three baskets of clothes and wallpapered almost every room in my house, but I see now that I have to forget the past and learn to give again. I can't hold you responsible for what happened to me before I met you. I can't expect you to let go of everything you've worked for just to make me feel important and good about myself. I feel pretty good about myself now, and I'm beginning to find out it's up to me to keep feeling that way."

"Kelly—"

"Let me finish. I rehearsed this whole thing last night while painting my garage."

"You painted your garage?"

"Yes. And I also realized I've got to get my love life in order so I can start sleeping nights again, but that's not important right now." She waved the matter aside and went on. "The important thing is I love you, and I'm willing to meet you halfway so we can have a life together. I just want your family to come first in your life, Macon. That's all I ask. I realize I can't expect you to be there for dinner every night, but in exchange I'd appreciate it if you didn't bring home your briefcase and open it up on the kitchen table each night." She realized she was fidgeting with her hands and sat on them. "I would like us to have time to sit on that porch you talked about building. I'd like you to play ball with Joey when you can, and be there to tuck Katie in once in a while, and help Samantha with her problems when she needs a man to talk to. And I'd like you to be at my side when our own babies are born."

She had to stop to catch her breath. Macon's expression gave nothing away. Had she, once again, made too many demands? Was he not willing to negotiate? He'd had two weeks to think about things and hadn't tried to contact her. Was it over as far as he was concerned? The thought made her want to throw herself prostrate on the floor and agree to anything.

"For heaven's sake, Macon, say something!" she cried.

Macon realized he was staring. The thought of Kelly carrying his child had jolted him to the soles of his feet. He was only beginning to see what wonderful things were in store for them. He took her hands in his and squeezed them. For a moment all he could do was gaze at the rather distraught face of the woman he loved more than life itself.

"Kelly, you aren't asking me for anything less than you deserve. I wanted to build a future with you, but it took a while for me to realize I had to rearrange my priorities. I wanted to come to you, but I needed time to get my life in order. I refuse to make promises I can't keep. Now I think I can offer you the kind of life you want . . . the kind of life you want for the children . . . the kind of life I want for myself."

His words relieved her so much, she actually felt weak. "And you're positive it's what you want?" She gazed up at him, searching his face. It had to be what he wanted.

He nodded. "More than you'll ever know." He brushed a kiss across her mouth. "Kelly, I thought I had everything until I met you. Then I realized I had less than I started out with." He looked hopeful. "Does this mean you'll marry me so we can start looking for that hound dog to put on our front porch?"

She laughed. "Yes, Macon." She'd barely gotten the words out of her mouth before he captured her lips in a heated kiss.

When he raised his head there was a pained look on his face. "You don't know how badly I've ached for you, Kelly. I can't eat or sleep. I wake up in the middle of the night in a cold sweat."

She stroked his jaw. "I think I do."

He felt his body respond to her simple touch. Not only did she have the power to stir his desires, she tugged every one of his emotions. He kissed her deeply, hungrily, but it was not enough. When he pulled away, he was trembling. "I could lock the door, you know. We'd have all the privacy in the world."

"I don't have much time left on my lunch hour, Macon. And I don't want to make my boss angry, since I'll probably have to ask for time off when we get married and all." Married to Macon. It had a nice sound to it. It was almost as nice as the way he was making her feel right now, all soft and mushy inside. A delicious warmth filled her lower belly. "And I really like my job, Macon," she went on, trying to pick up the thread of her conversation. "I'd like to work until we decide about having more children."

He nodded. "We can work it out, Kelly. I don't think there's anything we *can't* work out." He nuzzled his face against her neck as he spoke, taking delight in the feel and smell of her. There were so many things to discuss, so many plans to make, but for the moment nothing mattered except holding her in his arms.

"So how long do you have left on your lunch hour?" he asked.

Chills ran up her spine as his lips toyed with her earlobe. She glanced at her watch. "About thirty minutes."

He laughed. "Why, that's all the time in the world." He stood and crossed the room, then, smiling wickedly, he locked the door.

THE EDITOR'S CORNER

As you look forward to the holiday season—the most romantic season of all—you can plan on enjoying some of the very best love stories of the year from LOVESWEPT. Our authors know that not all gifts come in boxes wrapped in pretty paper and tied with bows. In fact, the most special gifts are the gifts that come from the heart, and in each of the six LOVESWEPTs next month, characters are presented with unique gifts that transform their lives through love.

Whenever we publish an Iris Johansen love story, it's an event! In **AN UNEXPECTED SONG**, LOVESWEPT #438, Iris's hero, Jason Hayes, is mesmerized by the lovely voice of singer Daisy Justine and realizes instantly that she was born to sing his music. But Daisy has obligations that mean more to her than fame and fortune. She desperately wants the role he offers, but even more she wants to be touched, devoured by the tormented man who tangled his fingers in her hair. Jason bestows upon Daisy the gift of music from his soul, and in turn she vows to capture his heart and free him from the darkness where he's lived for so long. This hauntingly beautiful story is a true treat for all lovers of romance from one of the genre's premier authors.

In **SATURDAY MORNINGS**, LOVESWEPT #439, Peggy Webb deals with a different kind of gift, the gift of belonging. To all observers, heroine Margaret Leigh Jones is a proper, straitlaced librarian who seems content with her life—until she meets outrageous rogue Andrew McGill when she brings him her poodle to train. Then she wishes she knew how to flirt instead of how to blush! And Andrew's

(continued)

(continued)

peaceful Saturday mornings are never the same after Margaret Leigh learns a shocking family secret that sends her out looking for trouble and for ways to hone her womanly wiles. All of Andrew's possessive, protective instincts rush to the fore as he falls head over heels for this crazy, vulnerable woman who tries just a bit too hard to be brazen. Through Andrew's love Margaret Leigh finally sees the error of her ways and finds the answer to the questions of who she really is and where she belongs—as Andrew's soul mate, sharing his Saturday mornings forever.

Wonderful storyteller Lori Copeland returns next month with another lighthearted romp, 'TIZ THE SEASON, LOVESWEPT #440. Hero Cody Benderman has a tough job ahead of him in convincing Darby Piper that it's time for her to fall in love. The serious spitfire of an attorney won't budge an inch at first, when the undeniably tall, dark, and handsome construction foreman attempts to turn her orderly life into chaos by wrestling with her in the snow, tickling her breathless beside a crackling fire—and erecting a giant holiday display that has Darby's clients up in arms. But Darby gradually succumbs to Cody's charm, and she realizes he's given her a true gift of love—the gift of discovering the simple joys in life and taking the time to appreciate them. She knows she'll never stop loving or appreciating Cody!

LOVESWEPT #441 by Terry Lawrence is a sensuously charged story of UNFINISHED PASSION. Marcie Courville and Ray Crane meet again as jurors on the same case, but much has changed in the ten years since the ruggedly sexy construction worker had awakened the desire of the pretty, privi-

(continued)

leged young woman. In the intimate quarters of the jury room, each feels the sparks that still crackle between them, and each reacts differently. Ray knows he can still make Marcie burn with desire—and now he has so much more to offer her. Marcie knows she made the biggest mistake of her life when she broke Ray's heart all those years ago. But how can she erase the past? Through his love for her, Ray is able to give Marcie a precious gift—the gift of rectifying the past—and Marcie is able to restore the pride of the first man she ever loved, the only man she ever loved. Rest assured there's no unfinished passion between these two when the happy ending comes!

Gail Douglas makes a universal dream come true in **IT HAD TO BE YOU,** LOVESWEPT #442. Haven't you ever dreamed of falling in love aboard a luxury cruise ship? I can't think of a more romantic setting than the *QE2*. For Mike Harris it's love at first sight when he spots beautiful nymph Caitlin Grant on the dock. With her endless legs and sea-green eyes, Caitlin is his male fantasy come true—and he intends to make the most of their week together at sea. For Caitlin the gorgeous stranger in the Armani suit seems to be a perfect candidate for a shipboard romance. But how can she ever hope for more with a successful doctor who will never be able to understand her wanderer's spirit and the joy she derives from taking life as it comes? Caitlin believes she is following her heart's desire by traveling and experiencing life to the fullest—until her love for Mike makes her realize her true desire. He gives her restless heart the gift of a permanent home in his arms—and she promises to stay forever.

(continued)

Come along for the ride as psychologist Maya Stephens draws Wick McCall under her spell in **DEEPER AND DEEPER,** LOVESWEPT #443, by Jan Hudson. The sultry-eyed enchantress who conducts the no-smoking seminar has a voice that pours over Wick like warm honey, but the daredevil adventurer can't convince the teacher to date a younger man. Maya spends her days helping others overcome their problems, but she harbors secret terrors of her own. When Wick challenges her to surrender to the wildness beneath the cool facade she presents to the world, she does, reveling in his sizzling caresses and drowning in the depths of his tawny-gold eyes. For the first time in her life Maya is able to truly give of herself to another—not as a teacher to a student, but as a woman to a man, a lover to her partner—and she has Wick to thank for that. He's shown her it's possible to love and not lose, and to give everything she has and not feel empty inside, only fulfilled.

Enjoy next month's selection of LOVESWEPTs, while you contemplate what special gifts from the heart you'll present to those you love this season!

Sincerely,

Susann Brailey

Susann Brailey
Editor
LOVESWEPT
Bantam Books
666 Fifth Avenue
New York, NY 10103

FOREVER LOVESWEPT

SPECIAL KEEPSAKE EDITION OFFER

$12^{95}

VALUE

Here's your chance to receive a special hardcover Loveswept "Keepsake Edition" to keep close to your heart forever. Collect hearts (shown on next page) found in the back of Loveswepts #426-#449 (on sale from September 1990 through December 1990). Once you have collected a total of 15 hearts, fill out the coupon and selection form on the next page (no photocopies or hand drawn facsimiles will be accepted) and mail to: Loveswept Keepsake, P.O. Box 9014, Bohemia, NY 11716.

FOREVER LOVESWEPT
SPECIAL KEEPSAKE EDITION OFFER
SELECTION FORM

Choose from these special Loveswepts by your favorite authors. Please write a 1 next to your first choice, a 2 next to your second choice. Loveswept will honor your preference as inventory allows.

_____BAD FOR EACH OTHER   Billie Green

_____NOTORIOUS   Iris Johansen

_____WILD CHILD   Suzanne Forster

_____A WHOLE NEW LIGHT   Sandra Brown

_____HOT TOUCH   Deborah Smith

_____ONCE UPON A TIME...GOLDEN
       THREADS   Kay Hooper

Attached are 15 hearts and the selection form which indicates my choices for my special hardcover Loveswept "Keepsake Edition." Please mail my book to:

NAME:_____

ADDRESS:_____

CITY/STATE:_____ZIP:_____